PALEOJOE'S
DINOSAUR DETECTIVE CLUB

BOOK #2

STOLEN STEGOSAURUS

with Wei

D1502620

Mackinac Island Press
for the love of reading

MYS
J
KCH

Other PaleoJoe Books

Dinosaur Detective Club Chapter Books

#1 The Disappearance of Dinosaur Sue
#3 Secret Saber-Tooth
#4 Ripping Raptors
#5 Mashing Mastodons

Hidden Dinosaurs

...and more to come...

First Edition

Library of Congress Cataloging-in-Publication Data (on file)

PaleoJoe's Dinosaur Detective Club #2: Stolen Stegosaurus

Summary: PaleoJoe, his eleven-year-old assistant Shelly, her classmate Dakota, and Detective Franks go on a dinosaur dig, where Shelly makes a rare find and Dakota goes undercover in an attempt to foil a plot to steal fossils.

ISBN 1-934133-04-3
ISBN 13 978-1-934133-04-0

Non-Fiction
10 9 8 7 6 5 4 3 2 1

Printed and bound in the United States
A Mackinac Island Press, Inc. publication
Traverse City, Michigan

www.mackinacislandpress.com

*Dedicated to the imagination
and discovery that
all children have with dinosaurs.*

STOLEN

STEGOSAURUS

TABLE OF CONTENTS

TABLE OF CONTENTS

CHAPTER ONE

THE FATE OF ALL THIEVES

Dakota Jackson was in trouble. Again.

It was the last week of school. Jeremy Maxwell's red and blue Superman pen with the light up eraser on it was missing. Jeremy blamed Dakota for taking it. In the past, Dakota had not been innocent in situations like this. Because of this his teacher had sent him straight to the principal's office.

Mr. DeLozo's office was large and had huge windows. There was nothing in it—including Mr. DeLozo himself—that Dakota liked. Dakota felt very small as he sat on the hard brown chair. Trying not to look too concerned, Dakota tried not to look at the walls. They were a freaky blue color that reminded him of the mold you sometimes see on cheese. They were covered with about a hundred framed snapshots of Mr. DeLozo with famous, or sort of famous, people.

And then there was the Punishment Board. Dakota was also familiar with that. Too familiar.

Mr. DeLozo let *The Silence* settle in as he frowned at the boy sitting in front of him.

Dakota knew all about *The Silence*. Mr. DeLozo used it to scare kids into saying what they had done wrong. It usually worked on Dakota, tough as he was. But today there was a little problem.

Dakota wasn't guilty.

Dakota tried to distract himself by looking at some of the snapshots on the wall behind Mr. DeLozo's broad shoulders. There was a picture of Mr. DeLozo in a pair of shorts that showed way too much of his pale and chubby legs, shaking hands with Mickey Mouse.

The Silence continued.

It was getting warm. Maybe the air conditioning was broken.

More *Silence*.

"I didn't do it!" Dakota exclaimed, *The Silence* breaking him at last. "I really really promise you, Mr. DeLozo, that I didn't take that pen!"

"Really?" Mr. DeLozo raised thick eyebrows and looked as though he did not believe a word Dakota was saying.

"Look, I know that in the past I may have borrowed..."

"Stolen," Mr. DeLozo corrected.

"Borrowed," Dakota insisted. "But not this time! I swear it!"

"Well," Mr. DeLozo opened his desk drawer and took out a dart with a blood red feather on it. "I don't think your teacher would have sent you to me if there had been any doubt."

He handed the dart to Dakota.

"You know what to do."

With a sigh Dakota took the dart. I suppose this is the fate of all thieves, he thought to himself.

On the back of Mr. DeLozo's big office door hung a dart board. Instead of numbers in each block, there were punishments. There were all sorts: *clean blackboards, no recess, scrape gum*, and, the very worst one in Dakota's mind, *stay after school.*

Dakota took careful aim. He would try for cleaning blackboards. Sometimes you could have a bit of fun doing that one. He would throw on three.

One...

Two...

The knock at the door was so quick that neither Mr. DeLozo nor Dakota actually heard it.

Three...

The door opened. The dart flew through the air straight at the girl who stood unprepared in the doorway!

CHAPTER TWO

THE RESCUE

Thunk!

The dart buried itself in the back of the book the girl held in her arms.

"OH!" yelped the girl.

"I'm sorry!" Dakota rushed forward. He knew this girl! It was his classmate, Shelly Brooks, the one who knew all about dinosaurs and fossils and things. "Are you hurt?"

"No, I'm not hurt," Shelly said, pulling the dart from her book and tossing it on the floor. "But you put a hole in my book!"

"I didn't mean to," Dakota tried to apologize. What was Shelly doing here? Shelly,

Dakota knew, was not the type of girl to ever be found in the principal's office. She was the sort of girl who did everything right. She never got in trouble. She always did her homework. She got straight A's. She was also the kind of girl who never paid any attention to boys like Dakota.

"Shelly," Mr. DeLozo began to scold. "You should never barge into my office in that way!"

"I don't barge," said Shelly, marching up to his desk. "I knock and enter."

"Well, you should knock and then wait for someone to invite you in. That's manners," said Mr. DeLozo.

"Well, of course I know about manners," said Shelly with great pity in her voice. "But I knew that if I stood around waiting for you to invite me in, Dakota would get his punishment and then you would have to do all sorts of apologizing."

"Apologizing?" Mr. DeLozo's eyebrows seemed to wiggle across his forehead as he struggled to understand the stream of words being hurled at him. Dakota just stood to one side, his mouth slightly opened, wondering if he could slip away without anyone noticing.

"Dakota, stay where you are!" Mr. DeLozo shouted.

"And, anyway, as it turns out, you will

have to apologize after all," Shelly continued as though no interruption had taken place. "Because Dakota did not take Jeremy's pen. Here it is!"

And she tossed onto the desk a red and blue Superman pen with a light-up eraser.

"That dim brain let me use it for social studies and then forgot I had it. Only Jeremy could be so forgetful," said Shelly, rolling her eyes.

"Told you I didn't take it," said Dakota.

"Yes, well…" Mr. DeLozo took the pen and quickly put it in a desk drawer. These sorts of things always caused trouble. Best to put it away, he thought.

"So, please apologize to Dakota because the last bell rang about 10 minutes ago and I'm going to be late to the museum."

"Right. Sorry, Dakota. I guess you did not take Jeremy's pen after all."

"Good," Shelly examined the pinpricked hole in the back of her book. "Oh well," she shrugged. "It's just a math book."

And with that she spun around and ran out of the room. Her short, red ponytail bounced merrily behind her.

This time *The Silence* was not planned. Dakota stood blinking at Mr. DeLozo. Mr. DeLozo blinked back.

"See you tomorrow Mr. DeLozo," said Dakota when he thought it might be safe. He picked up his backpack and quickly covered the length of the room to the door before Mr. DeLozo changed his mind about letting him go.

"Right," said Mr. DeLozo to the disappearing backpack of Dakota Jackson.

Was that a small tornado of righteousness or an 11 year old girl? DeLozo wondered as the door closed softly behind the departing Dakota.

The hallways were deserted. Dakota ran the whole length. He burst out of the front doors and let them slam behind him. Just down the sidewalk from the school he could see Shelly Brooks.

"Hey, Shelly!" he shouted. "Wait up!"

Waiting for Dakota Jackson was the last thing Shelly Brooks wanted to do. Getting him off the hook for the disappearance of Jeremy's pen had been the right thing to do, but she did not want to encourage a friendship with this particular boy.

She pretended she didn't hear him and began to walk faster.

"Hey! Wait!" Dakota put on the speed and caught up to her. Shelly had to admit he was a pretty fast runner, but now what? Now she would have to be nice.

"Oh. Hi Dakota," Shelly said, and maybe her smile was not truly genuine as she greeted him. "You don't have to thank me or anything. I mean, I just spoke up because I had that pen and I didn't want you to get into trouble for something you didn't do."

"Well, thanks anyway." Dakota fell into step beside her. "Are you heading home? Can I walk with you?"

"I'm not actually going home right now. I'm going to the Balboa Museum. That's probably out of your way. It's okay—I'll see you at school tomorrow." She began to walk a bit faster.

But it wasn't going to be that easy.

"The Balboa! Great! I live about a block away from there. I'll walk with you," said Dakota. He easily matched her speed.

So Shelly had no choice. That's why when they got to the Balboa Dakota followed her inside. Shelly had no idea how to get rid of him.

CHAPTER THREE

ENTERING THE TOMBS

Squeeeky—Creeeeak! Squeeeeky—Creeeeak!

"Wow!" exclaimed Dakota as he and Shelly walked down the old staircase to the lower levels of the museum. "These stairs are awesome! Listen to the way they creak and groan. This is so cool!" And he ran back up several steps in order to creak his way down them again.

Shelly had to smile. She also loved the creaky music of these old stairs.

"Where are we going again?" asked Dakota, catching up to her.

"The Tombs," said Shelly.

"Right. Is that where they keep mummies and things?"

"Hardly," Shelly laughed. She thought about how a friend of hers, who spent an awful lot of his time in the Tombs, would feel to be thought of as a mummy.

"So what's down here?"

"Follow me. I'll show you." Shelly led Dakota all the way to the final level. There they were stopped by a door. It was locked. Shelly knocked on it in a strange and special rhythm. Three short fast knocks, one long and slow knock, and five super-fast knocks.

The door opened. The tall figure of Bob, the chief of maintenance, appeared. Through the tangle of his black beard, he frowned at the two kids.

He looks like Blackbeard the Pirate, thought Dakota. He wondered if Shelly knew what she was doing.

"No one enters the Tombs unless they can answer my question," the man boomed in a very loud and, to Dakota, somewhat scary voice.

"Who is this guy?" he muttered in Shelly's ear. "And, by the way, do you know any Kung Fu or stuff?"

Shelly smiled. "Go ahead," she said to the man. "Ask away."

"What does the name *Tyrannosaurus Rex* mean in Greek and Latin?"

For a minute Shelly looked a little surprised. Then she leaned close to Bob and whispered, "That's sort of really easy, isn't it?"

"I thought maybe your friend might want a go," Bob whispered back.

"Gosh," said Shelly in a normal tone. "Do you know the answer, Dakota?"

"What if I don't?" asked Dakota suspiciously.

"Then NO ONE ENTERS THE TOMBS!" the man with the black beard rumbled.

"Okay, okay," said Dakota quickly. "As it happens, I do know the answer to this question. I remember it from that talk you and that dinosaur man gave at school after you guys solved that missing dinosaur crime."

Shelly was a bit impressed with Dakota. He was talking about a recent adventure. Shelly and her friend PaleoJoe had been called in to solve the mysterious disappearance of Dinosaur Sue. Who ever thought that a goof and show off like Dakota had ever paid any attention at all to things like that?

"May I have your answer, then?" Bob demanded.

"Sure," Dakota shrugged his shoulders. *Rule Number One: Never show you are concerned even when being stared at by giant*

men who look like pirates.

"*Tyrannosaurus Rex* means 'tyrant lizard king.'"

"Enter, brave explorers and search out the *Unknown!*" said Bob standing aside.

Dakota and Shelly edged past him. The door closed. They were standing in a long and deserted hallway. Their destination was a door at the very end of it.

"Race you!" said Shelly and took off at a fast run.

"Hey!" shouted Dakota, taken by surprise. He dashed after her.

Shelly Brooks was fast and this was her favorite sprint. But Dakota Jackson was faster and even with her head start, he still beat her.

CHAPTER FOUR

PALEOJOE

Shelly and Dakota reached the huge battered oak door at the end of their sprint. They heard a sudden, giant crash and a muffled yell coming from the room beyond.

Quickly, Shelly opened the door. The two kids burst into the room.

It was a sight that easily overwhelmed Dakota. The office he found himself in was always, at least in disarray and at most, a complete mess. There were dinosaur and other fossil books scattered on the floor, and on shelves, and piled high on chairs. Paper coffee cups from local coffee shops were scattered around like leaves

from a tree. Dusty bones and bits and pieces of mysterious shapes lay scattered about as though some careless giant had discarded the bones from his dinner. And everything was covered with a layer of dust.

Dakota sneezed.

"Gesundheit!" Was that actually someone under that huge desk in the corner? Dakota blinked his eyes. He cautiously stepped closer for a better look.

"PaleoJoe, are you all right?" Shelly was down on her knees peering at the figure under the desk. It was like looking into the mouth of a cave. There was a lot of room under that ancient desk.

"Yes, Shelly. I'm fine," the man under the desk said grumpily. As he tried to look up at Shelly he banged his head on the bottom of the desk. "Ouch! Raptor claws and mammoth tusks! This is not fun!"

"Then what are you doing under there?" Shelly was giggling.

"Stop laughing. I just dropped this box of rocks and some of them rolled under here. Help me get them, will you?"

"Sure," Shelly quickly crawled under the desk. "Here, Dakota, take this, will you?" A hand snaked back out holding a collection of assorted

rocks. Dakota took them and set them on the desk. As Shelly and the man under the desk retrieved the rocks, they handed them to Dakota who arranged them carefully on the desktop.

They were strange looking rocks. They all had some interesting sort of imprint on them. Dakota had never seen anything like them before.

"There," the man grunted. He rolled out from under the desk. Shelly scrambled out after him. She was covered with dust and cobwebs. As she brushed herself off, Dakota sneezed again.

"PaleoJoe, this is Dakota Jackson. He's

one of my classmates," Shelly did introductions. "Dakota, this is PaleoJoe, Dinosaur Detective."

"Pish!" said PaleoJoe. "Hi there, young man."

Dakota recognized this man in his olive pants and khaki shirt as the person who had come to the school with Shelly. Now, he too had cobwebs festooned in his short, graying beard which he brushed away before offering his hand to Dakota.

"It's nice to meet you," said Dakota, shaking hands. *Rule Number Two: Always be polite, especially if you think you might be dealing with crazy people.*

"So, PaleoJoe," said Shelly, "what are all these rocks anyway?"

"These," said PaleoJoe, immediately focusing on the rocks as though they were something precious, like gold or diamonds, "are a special kind of fossil. Here, take a look."

He handed a smaller rock to both Shelly and Dakota. He also handed a sort of funny magnifying glass to Dakota.

"It's a loupe," said Shelly. "Use it like this." She demonstrated the use of the powerful little magnifying glass by holding it up to her eye and looking through it, viewing the fossil.

Dakota studied the rock he held. He

thought that he had never seen anything so fascinating in all his life. Imprinted on the surface of the rock were the forms of strange little creatures that looked like something from a science fiction story. Most of them were an oval leaf-shape with a strange helmet-like head and what appeared to be eyes placed on the top. Feathering out from the worm-like center of the body were appendages that looked like the thousand legs of a millipede. In fact, the small creatures on the rocks reminded Dakota of a cross between horseshoe crabs and the tiny sow bugs, or pill bugs he sometimes found around the old foundation of the school.

"Are these things real, or did you make them somehow?" he asked.

"Did I make them somehow?" PaleoJoe glared at Dakota. "*Apatosaurus* toes, young man! What you are holding in the palm of your hand is the fossil of a creature that existed in the ancient seas on this earth over 300 million years ago."

To Dakota, who thought that 30 years sounded ancient, 300 million was a little tough to get his head around. "And so, what are you saying?" he asked confused.

"They're trilobites, silly," said Shelly running her finger along the bumpy surface of

27

one. "They are the key creatures of the Paleozoic era."

Dakota scowled. How did she know so much?

"Go ahead, PaleoJoe," urged Shelly. "Explain it to him."

CHAPTER FIVE

THE TROUBLE WITH TRILOBITES

"Absolutely," said PaleoJoe. He sounded like a boy who had just been granted his favorite wish. "Now look, Dakota. Here are two different kinds of trilobites. What do you notice about them?"

PaleoJoe handed Dakota two rocks. On one Dakota saw that the little trilobite had rolled up into a tiny ball exactly like the pill bugs did on the playground when you poked them with your finger. The other fossil was on a wonderfully smooth rock that fit perfectly in the palm of

Dakota's hand. The imprint of the tiny creature on this rock showed the trilobite flat.

Dakota described all this to PaleoJoe who nodded eagerly.

"Exactly right!" he said. "Now, why do you think the creatures look this way?"

"You know you don't have a clue," said Shelly. "It's best to just say so."

"I don't have a clue," said Dakota.

"Of course you don't," said PaleoJoe happily. "That's why I'm going to have to tell you! First, you must remember what I always say. Shelly?"

"You always say," said Shelly, "that nature doesn't change."

"Correct!" shouted PaleoJoe. "And so we know that the trilobites are related to things like lobsters and pill bugs. And we know that whenever they felt in danger, they would roll themselves up into a ball to protect themselves."

"Like the pill bugs on the playground!" said Dakota. He was excited to know that he had thought of something and it turned out to be right.

"Precisely. We also know that they lived in clean water. The little rolled up trilobite is called *Phacops*. Among other places, they are found in Sylvania, Ohio. Now, picture to yourself the Devonian period of time. There is little life on land. The only forms of plants are very primitive ferns and club mosses. There are no real trees or flowers and so there is nothing to hold stuff to the ground.

"When hurricanes happened, the wild winds churned up the water. The land flooded and dirt washed into streams and rivers. This sediment is called slurry. It was washed into lagoons and oceans where the trilobites lived. The little trilobites rolled themselves up in a ball and then found themselves trapped under several feet of slurry. They could not unroll."

"Wow," said Shelly. "Those must have been some storms!"

"So, what about the ones that are flat?" asked Dakota.

"Those are called *Dalmanites*," said PaleoJoe. "They are found in Middleport, New York. And when you find them, not only are they flat, but they are also often pointing northeast."

"That's mysterious," said Dakota interested.

"Very," smiled PaleoJoe. "But, as with everything, there is an explanation. During the time of these trilobites, there was a volcano in what is now Canada. It erupted. When the ash

from the explosion fell into the water it poisoned it. The trilobites, who like clean water, died. When they died, they flipped upside down in the water because their top side was heavier.

"The water currents ran from the northeast. The currents ran over the trilobites until they oriented, or pointed, to the path of least resistance. That put their nose into the current."

"Amazing," said Dakota. He really liked the feel of the rock with the imprint of the little *Dalmanites* on it. He thought he sort of understood about that path of least resistance too. It was like how you allowed someone to accuse you of stealing—even when you didn't—because it was easier than fighting for the truth.

This poor ancient cousin of the lobster is really a lot like me, he decided. A creature that ended up on his head in the path of least resistance.

CHAPTER SIX

THE BORROW

"And so, Shelly," said PaleoJoe, as he began to put the trilobites away in another, sturdier box, "I assume you came down to check on our plans for the dig?"

Shelly nodded. "I just wanted to be sure I had a good list of everything. I don't want to forget to take something."

"What's a dig?" Dakota wanted to know.

"Oh, it's just something we paleontologists do," said Shelly with a superior shake of her head.

Dakota felt like an idiot. *Rule Number Three: Don't ask questions around annoying know-it-all girls.*

PaleoJoe noticed the look on Dakota's face. "Be civil, Shelly. One thing about paleontologists is that they love to talk about their work. Be glad someone is interested!"

"It's okay," Dakota shrugged. "Let me finish putting away these fossils. You guys can talk about your plans or whatever."

And so before PaleoJoe could protest, Shelly was dragging him away to another corner of the room. Dakota was left alone with the box of trilobite fossils. Carefully, he continued to place them in the new box. He couldn't help holding each one and looking at it before he let it go. One fossil in particular attracted him very much. It was small and brown and looked like the trilobite was staring directly out from the small rock right at Dakota. He liked the way it fit into the palm of his hand. He thought maybe he would like to keep it for awhile and look at it again later. So, making sure that PaleoJoe and Shelly were not looking, Dakota slipped it in his pocket.

It would be a *Borrow*. Dakota would bring it back in a day or so. No one would even know it was gone.

Dakota wandered over to where Shelly and PaleoJoe were talking. He really was curious to learn their plans.

The two were bent over a notebook. They were discussing things that were written in it.

"What's that?" asked Dakota, forgetting rule number three. He regretted it instantly when he saw Shelly roll her eyes.

Rule Number Four: Never forget Rule Number Three.

"These are my field notes," said PaleoJoe before Shelly could say something annoying.

"You write about fields? Like what? The grass and stuff?" Dakota really wanted to know. Personally, he liked baseball fields the best, but he also knew about corn fields and bean fields.

And that actually spelling the word 'field' gave him fits. It was one of those pesky *i-e* vowel things.

Shelly sighed. Boys could be pretty dim, she thought. She decided to let PaleoJoe handle it.

"Field notes are notes paleontologists write down in small notebooks. They describe the dig site." PaleoJoe, Shelly realized, was in his teacher mode. She shrugged listening with half her attention as she continued to browse the notes.

"Our notes contain important information like the size of the bones, the orientation—you know, which direction they face—how deep they

are in the dirt, who discovered them, and a lot of other information as well."

"Cool," said Dakota enthusiastically. "It's like a detective's notebook at the scene of a crime."

To understand Dakota, you had to understand his deep and obsessive love of crime. Feeling that he, himself, was a bit of an expert on capers and rule breaking, Dakota really did fancy himself more as one of the good guys. He wanted to be a detective someday. Shelly didn't know this about him. Neither did PaleoJoe, but PaleoJoe recognized enthusiasm when he saw it.

"I scribble my notes in pencil and sometimes in pen," PaleoJoe continued going into detail in face of Dakota's interest.

"And sometimes crayon," said Shelly, pointing to some purple scribble in the notes before her.

"Yes, well," PaleoJoe cleared his throat and stroked his beard in embarrassment.

"Hey," Dakota came to his defense. "It's important to get everything down. Sometimes you use what you've got to use to get the job done."

"Yes!" agreed PaleoJoe. "Very wise."

"Very difficult to read," muttered Shelly.

"So, what are these notes on?" asked Dakota.

That question caught Shelly's full attention. She wasn't sure she wanted Dakota to know all about this stuff. It was special. This dig was going to be her first dig. She didn't know how she felt about sharing that excitement with someone like Dakota. Shelly began very much to wish she had never marched into Mr. DeLozo's office.

Would PaleoJoe tell Dakota? She held her breath.

CHAPTER SEVEN

STEGOSAURUS SECRET

"Because you are Shelly's friend," said PaleoJoe, "I don't mind telling you what we are doing."

Shelly wanted to shout that Dakota Jackson was NOT her friend. She wanted to beg PaleoJoe to keep their secret. Before she could even think about how to prevent it, PaleoJoe was telling Dakota everything.

"We have found a very nice site where we have begun to excavate a large number of *Stegosaurus* bones. This summer Shelly will be coming along on the dig with us. It will be her first one, right Shelly?"

38

"Right." Shelly looked like she had just eaten something that tasted really bad. PaleoJoe did not seem to notice.

"Wow!" exclaimed Dakota. He really was impressed. "That sounds like so much fun! As far as dinosaurs are concerned, I've always kind of liked that *Stegosaurus* fellow with those armored plates and all."

And this was true. Dakota had started to learn more about dinosaurs ever since Shelly had begun to bring fossils and PaleoJoe into their classroom. Dakota liked the *Stegosaurus* because he had those big plates on his back and spiked tail.

"I like *Stegosaurs* too," said PaleoJoe. "They are one of the most popular species of dinosaur."

"Not a very smart dinosaur," said Shelly, thinking that, at the moment, PaleoJoe and *Stegosaurs* might have something in common. She was sort of upset.

"That's true," said PaleoJoe. "They were almost 30 feet long and their head was very small. Their brain was about the size of a walnut. There wasn't enough brain to coordinate that much body, so it had a ganglion in its hips to control the movements of its hindquarters."

"What's a ganglion?" asked Shelly.

Dakota was surprised. Was there something this girl didn't know?

"A ganglion is a sort of cluster of nerves. Some people call it a *Stegosaurus'* second brain. It wasn't actually a brain. It was a lot larger than his real brain," PaleoJoe explained.

"The most complete skeleton was found near Canon City, Colorado," said Shelly, as if to make up for not knowing what a ganglion was. "He was nicknamed Spike."

PaleoJoe laughed. "That's right," he said.

"And he walked on four legs," Shelly began.

"But his back legs were twice as long as his front legs," said Dakota interrupting her.

Shelly looked surprised and then annoyed.

"I know things too," said Dakota quietly.

"But you don't know enough to stay out of Mr. DeLozo's office," Shelly shot back.

"Pish!" said PaleoJoe. "No arguing now. Shelly, we'll be ready to go the day after school gets out. Do you have everything you need?"

"Yes!" Shelly was so excited that even Dakota couldn't ruin it for her.

"All right then. You two run along now and let me work on some things here."

"Thanks, PaleoJoe," said Shelly.

"Yeah. Thanks, PaleoJoe," said Dakota. "I really learned a lot here. Do you think I could come again sometime?"

Rule Number Five: If you want something, use good manners to get it.

"Of course," PaleoJoe smiled. "I love to talk about fossils."

And that was very true. Shelly and Dakota pinballed through the door. PaleoJoe could hear them scuffling and racing down the long hallway to the staircase.

Carefully, he put his *Stegosaurus* notes away. He would need them again very soon. He went over to the desk and hefted the box of trilobite fossils. He would need to find someplace—not his desk—to store them. As he looked around for a suitable place, he happened

to glance in the box. A sudden frown appeared on his face.

Was one of his fossils missing? He put the box down. He quickly sifted through the rocks. Yes, the little *Flexicalymene* fossil was gone.

For a moment he thought maybe it had been lost under the desk. He was just about to get down on his knees to crawl under the desk to look for it when he remembered handing it to Shelly to look at. No, it had definitely been with the group.

That meant that someone had taken it.

CHAPTER EIGHT

THE APOLOGY

Rule Number Six: When you do something wrong, the best thing to do is own up to it. Excuses make you weak.

Dakota knew this rule by heart. He had learned it from his dad who was always doing something wrong and then trying to blame it on someone else. It was why Dakota's mom had finally asked his dad to leave.

Dakota knew that he should not have borrowed PaleoJoe's fossil without asking. And the more he thought about it, the angrier with himself he became. PaleoJoe had been very nice to Dakota. He had told him about a lot of really

interesting things. He had treated Dakota like he was someone smart—like someone who could understand things. Someone like Shelly Brooks. That was a new experience for Dakota.

Dakota said good-bye to Shelly on the steps of the Balboa Museum and began his walk home alone. That's when he started to think about what he had done in borrowing the trilobite fossil without asking permission.

He fingered it in his pocket. He did like the weight of it there. He felt that it was special. But he also knew it wasn't his.

He was almost home when he decided that he would have to take it back. He looked at his watch. It was ten minutes to five o'clock. The Balboa closed at five.

Turning around, Dakota put on the speed. He ran like the wind. The warm air pushed against his face as though trying to slow him down. Dakota ran harder. He pounded up the steps to the museum and almost collided with Gamma Brooks as she emerged from the big front doors. Her arms, as usual, were full of books. Dakota blasted by her like a small missile. She frowned at him over the tops of her glasses as she balanced the books his war-like passage had upset. But she didn't scold him because she had heard him apologize for his rudeness as he catapulted past and understood it was an emergency.

Rule Number Seven: Always apologize for rudeness unless you are being rude on purpose to some baboon brain who is trying to clobber you for your lunch money. Then *Rule Number Eight* kicks in which is *always insult your enemy.*

Dakota sprinted for the stairs to the Tombs. He vaulted down them so fast the creaks and squeaks barely had time to speak before he hit the bottom. Then he discovered that the door

45

to the long hallway was locked.

He pounded on the door with his fist. He was a little surprised when it opened.

"Yes?" It was Bob. "I'm sorry but this level is off limits to visitors. Besides, the museum is closing now."

"I'm not a visitor," Dakota gasped. "Remember? I was here with Shelly just awhile ago. I need to see PaleoJoe. Is he still here?"

"Oh, right," said Bob a smile twitching his beard. "I remember. Sure, I think PaleoJoe is still in his office. Go ahead."

"Thanks!" Dakota streamed by him and sprinted down the long hall.

When Dakota burst into his office, PaleoJoe was again going over his *Stegosaurus* notes. Dakota's sudden entrance startled him.

"Well," he said recognizing Dakota. "I thought you might be back."

"Why? Why did you think that?" asked Dakota. Did PaleoJoe know he had taken the fossil?

"Because I invited you," said PaleoJoe. "Only I didn't expect you back so soon. Something on your mind?"

"Umm, yeah," said Dakota. These things were never easy!

He walked over to PaleoJoe's desk and

taking the trilobite fossil from his pocket, he placed it on the large dirty field notebook.

"I borrowed this," he explained. "Without asking."

There was a moment of silence while PaleoJoe looked first at the fossil and then at Dakota. "I see," he said.

Dakota waited for the yelling to start. But PaleoJoe did not yell. Instead he picked up the fossil and examined it.

"It's quite a fossil, isn't it?" he asked.

"Yes," Dakota agreed.

"I remember when I found it," said PaleoJoe. "I was out with some friends exploring for rocks in southern Ohio. You know, geologists use trilobite fossils as index fossils to date the age of rocks."

"I didn't know that," said Dakota.

PaleoJoe cradled the tiny fossil in his large hand. "It feels good in the palm of your hand, doesn't it?"

Dakota nodded miserably. Why didn't this man just yell at him and get it over with?

"I can understand, actually," said PaleoJoe, "why you would want to take this. You are not the first person to be bitten by this particular desire. Of course, some people go right ahead and steal fossils. They sell them on the black market. They

47

do it mostly for money. And some people spend hours under the hot sun digging in dirt with sweat dripping in their eyes and insects biting the back of their necks looking and looking for things like this."

PaleoJoe paused allowing Dakota a minute to understand what he was saying. "Which kind of person are you?" he asked.

Dakota didn't even have to think about it. "I'm the sort that likes to dig," he said. "I like to find out about things. I like to dig in mysteries and I like to know about stuff. I am so NOT that other kind! I'm really really serious. And I'm really really sorry I took the fossil."

"Well," said PaleoJoe. "I know that is true, otherwise you would not have brought it back."

He took the *Flexicalymene* and carefully returned it to the box of trilobite fossils he had stashed under the large desk. Dakota watched regretfully. Already he missed the friendly weight of it in his pocket.

"I have an idea," said PaleoJoe. "How would you like the opportunity to find your own fossil?"

"Really?" Had Dakota heard him right?

"Of course, really. I think we could use another digger on this *Stegosaurus* dig. Would you like to come with us?"

"Would I like to come with you?" he said. To Dakota it was like winning the jackpot of all jackpots. "Are you kidding!? That would be so great!"

"That's settled then," said PaleoJoe. "You'll need to get permission from your parents..." He dug in a drawer and handed Dakota a form that he used for students who wished to accompany the team on a dig. Shelly had had to fill out one just like it. "And since you are a friend of Shelly's, I think this is a very good idea!"

Dakota agreed with all his heart. But he did not tell PaleoJoe about the true lack of friendship between he and Shelly.

"By the way," he said. "Just where is it we are going?"

"South Dakota," said PaleoJoe.

And Dakota felt his heart begin to sing.

CHAPTER NINE

SPIKE

It took forever for the last few days of school to get over. Shelly thought she might pop she was so excited. She was busy too. She had to gather all her stuff together to get ready for the dig in South Dakota. It was going to be hot and dirty. She had to have the right gear.

She set about packing her pink backpack with all the essential tools she had as a budding paleontologist. These tools included a magnifying glass, a floppy hat with pink flowers to shade her eyes from the sun, a notebook and pencils, a very special book given to her by Detective Franks after their last adventure, and her space-age cell phone. But what she didn't have yet was the essential tool roll. Someday, Shelly promised herself, she would get a tool roll just like the one PaleoJoe had. It would have all the pockets and flaps, just like his, to carry all the special chisels and brushes a real paleontologist needed.

She also packed a bag of clothes and dug out her sleeping bag.

She was so busy that she did not have time to visit PaleoJoe. But, above all, she worked hard to avoid Dakota Jackson. That turned out to be not so hard as it appeared that Dakota was trying to avoid her as well.

Finally, the day of departure arrived. Shelly was to meet PaleoJoe on the front steps of the Balboa Museum. As she stood waiting for him, she looked up to see an amazing sight. A person was walking up the steps toward her. At first she didn't recognize that it was Dakota.

Dakota was dressed in khaki shorts, a white tee shirt, and red sneakers. Over his shoulder was slung an old black backpack. It seemed to hold so much stuff, it threatened to burst open. Carefully rolled on top was a green sleeping bag. Tucked under his arm was a battered notebook. He had a pencil stuck behind his ear. But the most extraordinary thing of all was on his head.

Dakota had spiked his hair. Thick with

hair gel, it stood straight up in rows of spikes. It gave Dakota's face a surprised look.

But all the surprise was on Shelly's part, not Dakota's.

"Hi," said Dakota as he came up to stand beside her. "Just call me Spike."

Shelly, maybe for the only time in her entire life, was at a loss for words.

Just then a red car with a dinosaur crossing sticker in the back window, pulled up by the curb. PaleoJoe got out.

"Hi, you two! Let's get going, then!" he called.

"Surprise!" said Dakota to Shelly. He ran down the steps to PaleoJoe who had opened the trunk of the car for the backpacks and gear.

Was it possible, Shelly wondered, that Dakota was coming with them? How could that be? Maybe she was really home still in bed and this was a bad nightmare.

But it wasn't a nightmare. PaleoJoe took Dakota's gear and stowed it in the trunk. She watched as Dakota calmly got into the back seat of the car.

"Hey, Shelly," PaleoJoe grinned at her as she handed him her gear. "I've got a surprise for you! I've invited someone along that I know you will be happy to see."

"How could you, PaleoJoe?" Shelly wailed. She tried hard to fight back angry tears. "This was supposed to be MY dig. Why did you have to spoil it and ask HIM along?"

"I wasn't really asked, you know," said a familiar voice behind her. "But I didn't mean to spoil your fun."

Shelly spun around. Leaning on the hood of the car was her friend, Detective Franks. And he did look very glum. Dressed in shorts, a tee shirt, and a baseball cap, he did not look very much like a detective at all.

"Detective Franks? Are you coming too?"

In their last adventure together, as they hunted for the person responsible for the disappearance of Dinosaur Sue, Shelly had come to respect and like Detective Franks as much as he had come to respect and like Shelly. She really was glad to see him.

Detective Franks sighed. "Yeah. My chief thinks I need to know more about how a dig works if I am going to track down fossil thieves."

"Shelly, I don't understand your reaction here," said PaleoJoe. "What's going on?"

"I'm sorry," said Shelly. "I didn't know you were talking about Detective Franks. I thought you were talking about Dakota."

"Oh," said PaleoJoe. "Now I'm beginning to understand."

"I didn't know that you had invited him," Shelly explained.

"Well," said Detective Franks. "He can have my spot and I could go fishing, only I suppose my chief would find out and then I'd be in trouble."

"I thought it would be nice for you to have a friend along," said PaleoJoe.

"Dakota is not my friend," said Shelly fiercely. "He is a troublemaker and he is dishonest!"

"I think you may find out some things about Dakota if you give him a chance," said PaleoJoe.

Shelly wasn't happy about it, but she didn't see what she could do to change things. She would just have to ignore Dakota as best she could. She would not let him spoil this adventure for her.

PaleoJoe and Detective Franks got into the front seat of the car. Shelly slid into the back beside Dakota who had been waiting there away from Shelly's angry fireworks. He knew she would be upset when she found out he was going too.

"Here," he said, offering Shelly a candy bar.

"Thank you," Shelly mumbled as she accepted it.

Rule Number Nine: Get off on the right foot with a girl by giving her some of her favorite candy bar.

"Just stay out of my way and don't talk to me," Shelly said, but she ate the candy bar anyway. She was surprised when she enjoyed it.

CHAPTER TEN

CRAZY CHUCK

PaleoJoe drove them to a small airstrip just outside of town.

"By the way," said Detective Franks before they got out of the car. "I'm just Mr. Franks on this so called 'vacation' of mine. No one needs to know I'm a detective."

"A real detective?" asked Dakota. This was an exciting discovery! "Are you a real detective?"

"No, he's a fake detective," snapped Shelly. "He's made of plastic."

"Shelly!" There was a shade of warning in PaleoJoe's voice.

Shelly sighed. She would have to get over this or she was going to find herself in trouble. But what else could you expect to happen when you hung around someone like Dakota who was the King of Trouble?

"Detective Franks helped us with the disappearing Sue case," she explained to Dakota. "He's really pretty good at it too," she added.

"Thanks, Shelly," said Franks. "I had some help though."

"Anyway," said Shelly to Dakota, "Detective Franks does not want anyone to know he is a detective."

"Like he's undercover?"

Yeah, thought Franks to himself. It's like I'm undercover. That sounds a whole lot better than 'going back to school to pick up a few tips on paleontology' which is how the chief had put it. I think I might begin to like this spiky haired kid, he grinned to himself.

"Cool! Our very own undercover detective!" Dakota said. This trip was just getting better and better.

PaleoJoe and Franks unloaded the gear from the car. Everyone helped haul it out to the field where a small yellow plane was waiting for them. Beside the plane, wiping his greasy hands on an even greasier rag, was the pilot.

He was dressed in ripped jeans and wore a faded leather jacket. His wild hair stuck out from his head in a brown tangle, only sort of tamed by a green rubber band that held some of it back in a pony tail. He wore dark reflective sunglasses, so that when Dakota was introduced to him all he could see was his own spiky-haired reflection staring back at him.

"This is Chuck Buckingham," said PaleoJoe. "He'll be our pilot on this dig."

"Why do we need a pilot?" asked Shelly.

"You need a pilot, little girl, because without one it'd take you all year to walk the plains to your dig site," said Chuck Buckingham, chomping noisily on a piece of gum.

"Please don't call me 'little girl,'" Shelly barely controlled her temper. "My name is Shelly."

"Learn somethin' everyday, don't cha?" Chuck grinned.

When Chuck smiled like that he looked a little like a shark, thought Dakota.

"Mr. Buckingham will also be bringing in supplies and our mail," said PaleoJoe.

Shelly looked doubtfully at the plane. "In that?"

That had been on Dakota's mind too, but he hadn't wanted to say anything. The plane looked like it was put together with duct tape and chicken wire. He was almost sure that there was no way it could fly and if it happened to be that it *could* fly, then there was no way it could stay in the air.

"Look, little Miss," said Chuck, sticking his face so close to Shelly she could smell the stale mint of his gum. "This is a twin engine Britten-Normal Islander. They made 'em in Europe and there ain't no better plane for island hoppin' in the world. Of course we ain't doin' island hoppin' in the badlands, but I have been a bush pilot in Alaska more years than you been alive. I know how to fly this bucket like nobody's bizzness. Yeah?"

"Sure," said Shelly falling back a step.

"Come on, everyone," said PaleoJoe. "Let's load up."

The back two seats of the plane had been removed to make space for cargo. All the gear was piled in there. As they were working to stow their things, Shelly looked up to see a young woman approaching them.

"PaleoJoe," she said, tugging at his arm to get his attention. "Who is that?"

CHAPTER ELEVEN

BAD TO THE BONE

The young woman approaching was tall and tanned. Dressed like a digger, she too carried a backpack with a sleeping bag rolled tightly on top. She wore a wide-brimmed, yellow floppy hat. A long blond braid hung down her back.

"Hi, Karen!" PaleoJoe called, waving his hat in the air.

The young woman waved back.

"That's Karen Orchard," said PaleoJoe. "She is a graduate student helping us on the dig."

Shelly went forward to introduce herself and to help Karen stow away her gear. Chuck moved in as well.

61

"Mornin', Miss," he smiled. "Let me help you with that bag."

He reached out to take Karen's backpack. Before he could take it, Karen turned suddenly so that her large pack punched Chuck in the stomach.

"Oof," he said as the air was knocked out of him.

"Oh, terribly sorry," said Karen as though she really was, but Dakota, who saw the whole thing, knew she had backpack punched Chuck on purpose. Good for her, he thought. There was something about Chuck that was a little scary.

"Here, let me help you," said Shelly.

"Thanks," Karen smiled. "You must be Shelly. I've heard a lot about you and I can't wait to talk dinosaurs with you! I think we'll be sharing a tent."

"Great!" said Shelly. She liked the looks of Karen Orchard and she was always eager to discuss dinosaurs with someone.

"Okay. We're ready to load up!" said PaleoJoe.

PaleoJoe and Detective Franks sat in two of the seats. Karen and Shelly buckled into the other two. That left the co-pilot's seat for Dakota.

Great, he thought. Me and the gangster get

to fly this bucket of bolts and I get a front seat.

"Hop in, kid," muttered Chuck.

"Name's Spike," said Dakota, deepening his voice. He put on his sunglasses which were not sinisterly reflective and would, on occasion, allow the left lens to fall out.

"Yeah?" said Chuck with unexpected interest. "Call me Crazy Chuck." As he pushed up his sleeve, Dakota saw he had a tattoo of a snake twisting up the length of his forearm. Crazy Chuck saw him looking and grinning his shark's grin, he said, "We are bad to the bone!"

Uh-oh, thought Dakota wondering how smart it had been to try and impress a guy like Crazy Chuck. Dakota tightened his seat belt a notch tighter. *Rule Number Ten: When hanging with dudes who are bad to the bone, your seat belt can never be fastened too tight.*

Chuck tossed Dakota a pair of earphones. Surprised, Dakota put them on and discovered he could hear everything Chuck was saying.

As Chuck started the engines, the small plane vibrated and began to hum with action. In the seats behind him, Shelly and her new friend Karen were excitedly chattering together and pointing out the window. Detective Franks was chewing gum and looking out his side of the plane as well.

63

PaleoJoe was enjoying the whole thing. He really hated to fly in the big commercial planes, but he actually sort of liked flying in these smaller planes. There was always so much to see. And right now, he was very glad to see Shelly enjoying herself so much.

They taxied out to the rough runway, the plane jittering and grumbling. Chuck flipped some switches, tapped a gauge, and gave Dakota a thumbs-up.

"Bush 1," the tinny voice cracked over the headset Dakota wore. It was the control tower. "You are cleared to taxi on runway 25 east."

"Bush 1. Copy that." Chuck swung the plane around. They headed for the runway.

"Bush 1, ready for takeoff," announced the control tower.

Chuck grinned at Dakota and chomped his gum as though his jaw was a mechanical machine. His snake tattooed arm flicked here and there as he flipped more switches and thumped more dials. Dakota felt as though he had put his life in the hands of a maniac.

Chuck pushed the throttle forward and the plane trundled ahead down the long runway. In the distance, Dakota could see the chain link fence that surrounded the little airport. They were heading right for it.

Faster and faster the little plane rumbled along. Then suddenly Chuck pulled back on his stick. The nose of the plane pointed to the sky. The wheels left the tarmac, Dakota's stomach left his middle and floated up somewhere around his ears, and the clouds began to get closer and closer. Looking over his shoulder, Dakota saw the ground getting farther and farther away.

Soon the plane leveled off. Overhead the clouds were like a lid. It soon became apparent to Dakota that Chuck meant to fly under that cloud ceiling.

Just then the plane dropped about 20 feet. Dimly Dakota was aware that Shelly had yelled out something that sounded like 'yahoo!' and that the plane hadn't crashed and that this was actually sort of fun. It was like a roller coaster ride.

"Hang on!" sang out Crazy Chuck in the earphones. "We are bad to the bone!"

CHAPTER TWELVE

THE FLIGHT IN

Shelly looked out her window as the plane flew over the badlands. The ground below was a patchwork of color and texture. The land was flat and treeless. Hills dotted the landscape and Shelly could see gullies, ditches, and ridges. The land looked sun-baked and hot.

They were flying low enough so Shelly could even see herds of antelope and mule deer running, startled by the big shadow of the plane.

Behind her, PaleoJoe tapped her shoulder to get her attention. He had to almost shout to be heard, but there were some things he wanted her to know.

"One-hundred-and-forty million years ago, that flat landscape you see there was covered with thick vegetation and plants like ferns and soft leafy trees," he said.

"Really?" Shelly could hardly believe it.

"See those clouds?" PaleoJoe pointed.

Shelly nodded. Overhead the blue sky was now punctuated by billowy white popcorn clouds.

"Clouds like that deposited heavy rains that left muddy stretches where dinosaurs left their footprints. And sometimes there was no rain for long periods of time."

"Droughts," said Shelly nodding. She knew about droughts. Her uncle was a farmer. He had often told her what happened to his cornfields in times of drought.

"That's right," said PaleoJoe. "And then when it rained, sometimes the rivers would overflow their banks. Dinosaurs were attracted to the water, of course. You know how big they were."

"I bet they got pretty thirsty," said Shelly.

"Life and death struggles occurred around those ancient water holes," said PaleoJoe. "Fossils tell us those stories."

As they approached their destination, Chuck took the airplane in a slow turn over the

dig site so PaleoJoe could get an overall look at the dig from the air. As they flew over, the tiny figures of the crew stopped working. Looking up and shading their eyes they waved or tossed their hats in the air. PaleoJoe gave Shelly a big grin. Everything looked like it was running smoothly.

They landed on the small landing strip and the plane bumped and coasted to a stop. When the propeller stopped spinning everyone climbed out and claimed their bags and packs.

Shelly and Karen high-fived each other. When Dakota approached and raised his hand, Shelly ignored him, leaving him standing foolishly with his hand in the air.

Hoping no one had actually seen this snub, Dakota changed the gesture into a smoothing his hair move, but forgetting that his hair was spiked and not smooth, this didn't really work either.

Rule Number Eleven: Don't volunteer to make yourself look stupid.

A pickup, old, beat-up, and blue, bounced its way toward the group. Stopping in a cloud of dust, Fred Parkhurst, PaleoJoe's crew leader, hopped out and came to meet them.

PaleoJoe and Fred shook hands. There were introductions all around. Everyone tossed their gear into the bed of the pickup and clambered aboard. Fred drove them the short distance to the site. Heat and dust settled on everyone like a second layer of clothing.

When the truck stopped, everyone unloaded and headed for the tents where the rest of the crew was eagerly awaiting their arrival. PaleoJoe and Fred, momentarily left alone by the truck, had a quick, private discussion.

"I hope he works out okay," Fred said.

"Well, we won't worry about it," said PaleoJoe. "I've had assistants before who were less than useful."

"Yeah," said Fred. "It's just that there's something about this guy that I have to say I don't like."

"Never mind," said PaleoJoe. "Let's go meet everyone. I'm sure everything will be fine."

And because his unreliable sunglasses had popped a lens, Dakota, crouched on the other side of the truck looking for it, heard every word they said.

CHAPTER THIRTEEN

SHELLY BROOKS, PALEONTOLOGIST

As Dakota approached the camp, he saw Crazy Chuck talking with some skinny guy out by one of the dig holes. Maybe it was his imagination, but he thought he saw Crazy Chuck gesture in his direction. He hurried to catch up to PaleoJoe and Fred.

Shelly discovered that she and Karen would indeed, be sharing a tent. This was great! PaleoJoe grinned as the two of them scooted by deep in conversation about bones, and how you could tell a bone from a rock as you were digging.

"The fossils in this area are usually black in color," Karen was saying. "They make a slight *tink* sound when you hit them with a metal trowel."

"That's how you know you have a dinosaur bone," said Shelly, nodding in understanding.

"Come on, Dakota," said PaleoJoe, seeing the boy looking a little lost in the middle of all the bustle. "Just set your gear over there and we'll go meet the crew."

Dakota added his pack to a pile outside a large tent and hurried to catch up to PaleoJoe. The heat and light of the late afternoon sun was intense. Dakota was glad he had his sunglasses, useless as they were at times.

A nattering sound in the air was Crazy Chuck taking off in his plane. Dakota watched as the tiny plane dipped and twisted out of sight.

The crew was assembled at a long table under the shade of a large awning. It was like a tent without sides. Dakota followed PaleoJoe as he grabbed a couple of camp stools and motioned Dakota to sit.

"Hi, everyone," said PaleoJoe. "I'd like to introduce to you some special people I have brought with me. This is my assistant and young paleontologist, Shelly Brooks."

Shelly smiled, suddenly feeling a little

shy as everyone looked at her. She gave a little wave.

"This is Dakota Jackson, a classmate of Shelly's."

Dakota nodded his head and his sunglass lens popped out. A few people laughed. Shelly scowled. Dakota felt hot as he popped the lens back into place. The thing had so many fingerprints on it now he couldn't really see out of it anyway.

"And this is Mr. Franks who is here to learn as much as he can about a fossil dig," PaleoJoe managed to say without a smile, which was not easy. Detective Franks scowled, already feeling the sweat trickling down the inside of his shirt and not enjoying it.

"And Karen Orchard is our graduate student from Ohio State."

Karen smiled and waved, then winked at Shelly.

Fred Parkhurst stepped forward. "Welcome to everyone," he said. "As you know, the rest of us have been here for about a week. We've got the dig open and we've begun to work where we left off last season. For those of you who are just joining us, let me introduce the crew already here and working."

Quickly Fred introduced John and Mary Rodgers, who were dig volunteers from

Pennsylvania. John had light blond hair and a lobster-red sunburn. His wife, Mary, was dark and short and looked like somebody's mom. Dakota thought they were probably pretty nice people. But that isn't what he thought about the next person Fred introduced. It was the skinny man Dakota had seen talking with Crazy Chuck.

"This is Theodore Edward Kaskia III," said Fred and Dakota saw him glance at PaleoJoe as he made this introduction. "Theodore is PaleoJoe's assistant on this dig."

"I thought I was PaleoJoe's assistant!"

It was Shelly. There was instant silence among the group. The skinny man looked over at Shelly. There was a strange smirk on his face.

That girl, thought Dakota, has got to learn when to keep her mouth shut.

"Call me Buzzsaw," the man said. He was leaning against the tent pole and chewing on a toothpick. "You're just a little girl," he said to Shelly. "You're just here to play around in the dirt."

Oh no, thought Dakota as Shelly stood up and faced Buzzsaw.

"*What* did you call me?"

Yep, thought Dakota, if tigers could speak they would probably sound like that.

"Actually, Shelly, you are my assistant," said PaleoJoe breaking into the awkward situation that was developing. Buzzsaw's face turned a slow red as he straightened up from the pole. "But you, Theodore..."

"I told you. Call me Buzzsaw," the man said in a voice that was a far distance from friendly.

"Pish! Buzzsaw, then...in any case, you are my grad assistant and working for your grade and so on. Now everybody, I have an announcement to make."

Quickly PaleoJoe took everyone's attention

off Buzzsaw as he produced a mysterious bundle wrapped in golden wrapping paper and tied with a yellow ribbon.

"As everyone knows, Shelly Brooks has been my assistant, and a most valued one, on many recent adventures. This is her first real dig, but she is well on her way to becoming probably the world's youngest paleontologist."

He paused while everyone applauded. Everyone except Buzzsaw. Dakota wondered what was going to happen next.

"Shelly," said PaleoJoe, "this is for you."

He handed her the bundle. Nervous and excited, Shelly took it from him and unwrapped it. Everyone watched.

"OH!!" It was a gasp and a squeal and part shout because what Shelly held in her hands was her very own tool roll.

And it looked just like PaleoJoe's except it was pink.

CHAPTER FOURTEEN

STORIES AND S'MORES

The sky around the camp was streaked with the gold and amber pink of the disappearing sun. Distant hills were blue against the backdrop and deep shadows collected in the gullies and ditches of the dig site.

After supper everyone gathered around the campfire to talk and tell stories. Shelly and Karen produced chocolate, marshmallows, and graham crackers to make s'mores. The orange and red fire gave off a cheerful crackling light. Overhead, the sky was filled with a million brilliant pinpricks of stars.

John Rodgers produced a guitar. He and

Mary led everyone in a round of songs. Fred brought out a harmonica and the little group of people made some special music in the lost reaches of the badlands to celebrate their dinosaur discovery.

"This is a very special dig site," said PaleoJoe when the music ended. The firelight danced across his face making shadows dance in his beard. "In the long-standing legends of the Sioux Indians are stories of monsters that walked these badlands."

Dakota felt a shiver of thrill run up his spine at these words.

"We have been lucky enough," continued PaleoJoe, "to find the skeleton of one of these monsters and to find it complete. Usually this is not the case. Most of what we are used to finding are scattered bones."

"Scavengers are responsible for a lot of that," said Karen as she put together another s'more. "A scavenger would crunch up the bones it found and tear the body apart, scattering bones everywhere."

Nice, thought Dakota, trying to catch Shelly's eye as he melted his s'more. He wanted to tell her how cool he thought her tool roll was and to ask her if he would be able to look at it.

"And water action could scatter the bones too," added Shelly, expertly ignoring Dakota. "If

77

a dinosaur died in or near a rushing stream or river, then as the body decomposed the bones would break apart and flow with the water."

Show-offs, scowled Dakota, deciding that he actually hated girls after all. Involved with this thought, he burned his fingers on a piece of hot melted marshmallow and dropped his s'more in his lap.

"Better watch that, kid," Buzzsaw said coming to sit next to him. Dakota couldn't see him very well in the shadows, but the guy smelled like Dakota's old gym shoes—which wasn't a good thing. "Coyotes like the smell of chocolate and marshmallow," the man continued. "Might find yourself becoming a tasty midnight snack for a pack of howling scavengers, if you know what I mean."

Dakota didn't know what he meant, but he also didn't like the sound of it, nonsense or not. Quickly he cleaned up the smeary mess with his shirt tail. He heard the skinny man laugh quietly.

"The smallest and lightest bones traveled the farthest," said PaleoJoe. "That's why when we find bones we draw them, photograph them, and even take compass readings to see which way the fossils are oriented."

"What can all that information tell you?"

Mary Rodgers asked. Dakota thought it looked like maybe she was taking notes on what PaleoJoe was saying.

"Hey, kid," the skinny man nudged Dakota in the darkness. "Chuck tells me you're an all right kid. Your name is Spike, that right?"

"Um, sure," agreed Dakota.

"Call me Buzzsaw," the man said. "You and I may need to talk a bit later."

The man got up and, leaving the circle around the fire, disappeared into the darkness. Talk to him later? Not if he could help it, Dakota determined.

Able to breathe a little easier now that the air around him wasn't polluted by gym shoe smell, Dakota turned his attention to PaleoJoe. This turned out to be a good thing because suddenly PaleoJoe turned his attention to Dakota.

"Actually, Mary," he said, "I think that I can let Dakota answer that question."

Startled, Dakota looked up to see everyone looking at him. "What question?" he asked blankly.

"The fossil orientation in flowing water question, light bulb," said Shelly in a superior tone of voice.

Rule Number Twelve: You should always

pay attention to lectures even when you are being threatened by neanderthal types who smell like moldy shoes.

"You mean like the trilobites?" asked Dakota.

PaleoJoe nodded encouragement.

"Well, the way I understand it," said Dakota, "is that when the bones were put in the water the way they pointed..."

"The orientation," Shelly interrupted him.

"Yes. The orientation gives scientists an idea of which direction the water current was flowing."

"That's it," said PaleoJoe. "All bones act in a special way when water is flowing over them."

"Because bones point themselves in the path of least resistance," Shelly capped off the lecture.

"Wow," said Mary. "You two kids sure know a lot about all this."

"Well," said PaleoJoe. "It's getting late and we have a big day ahead of us tomorrow. I think we had all better turn in."

There was a general agreement to this. As the crowd broke up Dakota made a point of going nowhere near Shelly. But he wasn't sure she noticed because she seemed to be making just such an effort to avoid him.

CHAPTER FIFTEEN

LOST AND FOUND

Shelly was glad to get to the tent she was sharing with Karen. She was very tired from all the excitement of the day. She was also very annoyed with Dakota and his ridiculously spiked hair.

"Boys are really annoying, aren't they," she commented to Karen.

"Did you have someone specific in mind?" Karen asked.

"No," Shelly lied.

Karen smiled. "Well," she said. "Just between you and me and the stars in the sky, some boys can be *very* annoying!"

Shelly laughed. "Oh, I'm so excited about tomorrow," she said as she unrolled her sleeping bag.

"Yes," said Karen. "I can imagine you would be. Your very first dig, using your very own tool roll."

"I love my tool roll," said Shelly. "In fact, I think I will sleep with it under my pillow!"

"Good idea," said Karen. "It will bring you good dreams."

Shelly rummaged in her bag where she remembered putting her new pink tool roll. She couldn't find it. Puzzled, she carefully took everything out of her bag in case the tool roll had managed to settle into the bottom of her pack. But it wasn't there.

"Karen!" Shelly exclaimed in dismay. "My tool roll is gone!"

Two tents over was a bigger tent that would be shared by PaleoJoe, Detective Franks, Dakota, and Buzzsaw. Dakota found PaleoJoe and Detective Franks talking just outside the tent.

"Well, Dakota," said PaleoJoe. "What do you think?"

"This is great!" exclaimed Dakota. "It's like camping. We're going to have so much fun!"

"Until the digging starts," grumbled

Detective Franks.

"What do you mean?" asked Dakota.

Detective Franks looked like he was in pain. PaleoJoe laughed. "He means he really hates heat, insects, and monotony," he said.

"It won't be that bad, will it?" asked Dakota, suddenly feeling a little worried.

PaleoJoe clapped him on the back. "Not for those kinds of people who like to discover things."

Detective Franks made a sound that sounded like a man choking. This made PaleoJoe laugh again.

"Go on ahead inside the tent, Dakota," said PaleoJoe. "Franks and I will be in after we check around to make sure everyone is settled."

Inside the dimly lit tent Dakota began to unroll his sleeping bag. Already asleep in his corner, Buzzsaw was giving new meaning to his name. His snoring, Dakota thought, sounded just like someone buzz cutting wood. Dakota smiled grimly to himself over this idea. One thing he knew, he didn't like Buzzsaw one little bit.

As Dakota began to unroll his bag onto the short cot provided to the diggers, he was startled to discover something hard wrapped in the roll. Puzzled, he continued to unroll his bag trying to remember if he had put in an extra pair of shoes

or something. But when he got his bag opened and pulled out the object, he found to his utter horror and dismay, that he was holding Shelly's pink canvas tool roll.

Just then the tent flap opened and Detective Franks came in.

Before Dakota could even think to hide what he held, Detective Franks saw it. Frozen, Dakota stood staring at the detective looking as guilty as any thief anywhere who had ever been caught red-handed.

"I didn't take this!" Dakota managed to say at last.

Detective Franks lowered the flap of the tent. He casually walked over to Dakota. He gave Dakota the feeling of being a small and very caught boy. Dakota did not like this feeling at all. It was worse than anything he had ever experienced in DeLozo's office.

"Don't you mean you didn't 'borrow' it?" Franks asked, his eyes hard. "That's what all of them say, you know. Every thief I have ever interrogated all said they only 'borrowed' it. 'Detective Franks, I only *borrowed* this car I hot-wired and drove all over town.' Doesn't really wash with me kid."

Of course Dakota had never *borrowed* anything as big as a car, but unfortunately he recognized his own reasoning as it was thrown back in his face. He wondered if PaleoJoe had told Detective Franks about how he had *borrowed* the trilobite fossil.

"No! I didn't borrow it or take it or anything! You've got to believe me! I found it here wrapped in my sleeping bag." Dakota desperately wanted Detective Franks to believe him.

In the corner, Buzzsaw rolled over with a snort that sounded to Dakota suspiciously like a laugh, but he didn't seem to wake up.

Detective Franks looked hard at Dakota. Franks was a pretty good judge of character and he had decided early on that Dakota was an okay kid. He did not at all enjoy finding him in the apparent act of taking Shelly's tool roll. But there was something, Franks had to admit, in the face of Dakota and his serious brown eyes that prompted him to want to believe what Dakota was saying. If a person could just ignore that silly spiked hairdo...

"Tell me what happened," he said.

"Nothing happened, really," said Dakota. "I just came in here and started making up my bed to go to sleep and I discovered this wrapped in my bag. Look, why would I want to take this from Shelly? And when would I have been able to do it?"

Franks thought back to the evening around the campfire. He couldn't remember if he ever saw Dakota leave or not.

"Okay," he said. "I'll give you the benefit of the doubt. This time. What's important now is that this is returned to Shelly right away."

Dakota couldn't agree more and he was in the process of handing it to Franks to do that very thing when the tent flap exploded open. Shelly herself stormed into the tent.

"PaleoJoe! Someone has stolen my tool roll!" she said in full cry.

Buzzsaw sat bolt upright in his bed as though he had been electrocuted. He was just in time to see Shelly, see Dakota, holding her tool bag.

"Oh, you thief!" she cried, rushing forward and snatching her tool roll away.

"Shelly, I..." Dakota tried to explain, but a hard shove from Shelly sent him sprawling to the floor of the tent.

"Don't speak to me! Ever!" And clutching her tool roll tight to her chest, Shelly stormed out.

CHAPTER SIXTEEN

THE DIG BEGINS

The next day the digging began in earnest. Everyone was up very early. Karen made coffee and as a thin veil of fog burned away before the rising sun, the diggers gathered.

"Okay, Shelly," said PaleoJoe. "You and Karen are with me. Today we are going to teach you the technique of digging."

"Yes!" Shelly pumped her fist in the air. She was clutching her tool roll. All through breakfast Dakota had noticed that she never once set it down.

"Dakota," continued PaleoJoe, "you and Mr. Franks are in charge of making some

sketches. You can also check around to see how things are going generally."

Dakota looked over at Detective Franks wondering what he had told PaleoJoe about Shelly's tool roll. Maybe this was punishment. Maybe no one trusted him now.

"Everyone else continue with your areas."

Shelly knew from her reading and from talking to PaleoJoe that most fossil dig sites are set up in areas that are about three meters square. This is a measurement that allows one digger to dig in a specific area and explore it properly.

As she followed PaleoJoe and Karen over to their specified area, she untied her tool roll. The little metal tools and brushes were all tucked neatly in pockets or trapped beneath flaps. She couldn't help grinning as she looked at these tools that were her very own.

"They're beautiful," said Karen. "I remember when I got my first tool roll. It was better than learning to drive!" She laughed.

"Okay, Shelly," said PaleoJoe. "Here is where we will work today. Now, in softer sediment like this, what you want to do is use one of your smaller brushes or a trowel to scoop dirt into one of these dustpans. Then drop the dirt into this bucket."

"Don't fling it over your shoulder," said Karen.

"Of course not," said Shelly.

"We remove these layers of dirt and sand slowly and evenly, one millimeter at a time," said PaleoJoe.

"It takes patience," Karen warned.

"I'll probably have to practice that," admitted Shelly.

"When you get enough dirt in your bucket," PaleoJoe continued, "you will take it over to one of the sifting screens that are set up on those stilts over there." He pointed to a central location where, as he said, screens on stilts sprawled like an awkward wooden bird.

"I know what to do then," said Shelly. "You want to sift through the dirt and look for smaller fossils, right?"

"Right!" PaleoJoe grinned. You might find fossils of small bones, teeth, or plants."

"Everything tells us part of the story," said Karen.

"What if I find a bone?" asked Shelly.

"If a bone is discovered, it is left in place and we will continue to remove the dirt from around it. We will need to draw, measure, orient, and photograph it. If you find a bone, first call me over and then we'll call over Franks and Dakota to draw and photograph it."

"Okay, Shelly," said Karen. "You can start by sharing this space with me."

Shelly got down on her knees beside Karen. In the dirt a part of a femur, one of the large leg bones, was already partly exposed. Selecting a brush from her tool roll, Shelly carefully began to work. PaleoJoe watched her for a few minutes to be sure she understood what she was doing.

First, she carefully and slowly brushed some dirt into the dustpan. Then she emptied it into the bucket. As she repeated this process,

PaleoJoe nodded in satisfaction and moved off to check on others.

The shadow from Shelly's hat made a pool of shade on the bone fragment she worked on. Her concentration was complete. She worked slowly and carefully.

Watching her from a short distance away, Dakota was amazed at her patience. Already the flies had discovered that they enjoyed buzzing around his head. He was also pretty sure Detective Franks was annoyed by their attention as well. He was glad he had decided not to spike his hair because he had a suspicion that the flies would have loved his hair gel. Anyway, it was easier to wear a hat without spiked hair.

"Can you take photographs?" Franks asked him.

"Yep," said Dakota, remembering how he had taken a few snapshots one time on a disposable camera on a class field trip to a zoo. Most of the pictures had come out with Dakota's thumb, a large bald alien blob, right in the center of pictures of the elephants and giraffes. Well, Franks hadn't asked if he could take *good* pictures.

"And I can draw," said Dakota.

This was true. Dakota actually had a little bit of talent for drawing. Superheroes

were his specialty. Probably not a lot of call for superheroes on a fossil dig though, he thought.

"Here," Franks shoved the camera at Dakota. "Just point and click."

Dakota did as he was told. He pointed the camera at Detective Franks and clicked. He was amazed that the look Franks gave him failed to vaporize him into dust atoms where he stood.

This is the price of being clever with me, Dakota thought grinning back.

CHAPTER SEVENTEEN

THE FIND OF A LIFETIME

The afternoon wore on. The sun beat down on the diggers. PaleoJoe was beginning to feel a bit cramped as he crouched and bent over parts of the dig. He wore a bandana under his hat to help soak up the sweat. Once Dakota saw him pour some water over his head and bandana. He thought it looked like a great trick to cool off.

Shelly, now working on her own, seemed not to notice the heat, the flies, the dust, or really anything except the little patch of dirt she was scraping and brushing. Suddenly, as Shelly gently dug deeper and deeper around the bone she was working on, her trowel hit something and went *tink*.

"PaleoJoe, I found something! I found something!" she yelled.

PaleoJoe, who had just lowered himself down to look at a bone fragment Fred was working on, straightened up. His face was shaded by his big floppy hat. He was dust covered and very hot.

"What is it, Shelly?" he asked, walking over to the edge of Shelly's excavation.

"I don't know but it's black and it *tinks!*" said Shelly excitedly.

PaleoJoe crouched down to take a look. "I'm sorry, Shelly," he said. "That's just a pebble."

Shelly scowled down at her digging. "Drat," she muttered. "I thought for sure I had found something."

"A stone is something, little girl," said Buzzsaw who happened to stroll by just at that moment. He was carrying a bucket full of dirt over to the screens. "You aren't really expecting to find anything important, are you?"

Shelly frowned, darkly glaring at his retreating back. "You smell like a pile of dirty clothes," she said, but not loud enough for Buzzsaw to hear her.

Dakota heard her though, and he smiled because he agreed with her.

Shelly saw Dakota smiling and thought he was laughing at her. "Stay away from me," she said fiercely and ducked back down to her digging.

PaleoJoe sighed and motioned Dakota over to help him.

"I didn't take her tool roll," said Dakota to PaleoJoe. "I didn't borrow it either."

"It's okay, Dakota," PaleoJoe said. "You know, actually both Franks and I believe you. You'll just need to give Shelly some time."

Dakota felt relieved and frustrated at the same time. At least, he thought, Franks and PaleoJoe would be his friends. And Buzzsaw, he reflected gloomily, watching the skinny figure of the man bent over the screens sifting through the dirt. As he was watching, he suddenly saw Buzzsaw snatch something off the screen and put it in his pocket. Buzzsaw did it so quickly and so smoothly that Dakota wasn't sure he saw it happen.

"Hey, PaleoJoe," he said. "When a digger finds something as they sift through the dirt, what are they supposed to do with it?"

"Everything is labeled and tagged and a lot of notes are written up on it," said PaleoJoe. "The dirt and the stuff we find it in tell us the stories of the ancient times."

"And so you're not supposed to put something in your pocket if you find it," said Dakota just making sure of the matter.

"Definitely not," said PaleoJoe. "Why are you asking?"

"PaleoJoe!" It was Shelly again, so Dakota never had a chance to tell PaleoJoe what he had seen. "I think I found something!"

Dakota heard PaleoJoe say something that sounded like "Pish."

"She sure is excited about all this, isn't she?" said Dakota.

PaleoJoe grinned. "After all," he said, "this is what it is all about, isn't it?" He walked back over to Shelly. Dakota trailed behind. He wanted to know if Shelly found something cool, but he was also trying to stay out of her way.

"Look, PaleoJoe," said Shelly holding up a small piece of something. "I found this. It doesn't look like stone to me. Is it a fossil of some sort?"

PaleoJoe held out his hand for the object. When Shelly placed it in his hand he felt his heart give a little skip.

No, he thought, this can't be.

He tried to be calm, but it was as though a million butterflies were suddenly gathering in his gut. He took out his loupe and carefully, under the strong magnification of the little glass, he looked at Shelly's find.

Dakota cautiously peered over PaleoJoe's arm to see what he had. What PaleoJoe held in the palm of his hand was small, about the size of a quarter. It was black and had rough edges. It looked slightly convex to Dakota because it seemed to curve just slightly, sort of like the lens of his sunglasses. What Dakota couldn't see was that under the magnification of PaleoJoe's loupe, the surface of Shelly's find was textured with really tiny bumps.

"Well?" Shelly demanded impatiently. "Is it a fossil or isn't it?"

"Oh, Shelly," said PaleoJoe in a funny strangled sounding voice.

"PaleoJoe, are you all right?" asked Karen anxiously as she came up to stand by Shelly. "You're not having a stroke or something, are you?"

"No," said PaleoJoe still in his funny voice. "Shelly, are there any more fragments like this one?"

"Sure," said Shelly a little puzzled by PaleoJoe's behavior. "Look, Karen, you can see some of them for yourself."

Karen knelt down. She took her brush to carefully sweep away some dirt.

"Ohmigosh!" she exclaimed. "PaleoJoe, this isn't what it looks like, is it?"

"WHAT IS IT?" Shelly yelled in her power voice.

This not only caught everyone's attention, but it seemed to snap PaleoJoe out of his daze.

"Shelly," he said. "I think you have just made the discovery of a lifetime."

"Well, obviously," said Shelly. "Now please

tell me what it is I have found."

"Dinosaur eggs," said PaleoJoe, feeling suddenly that he needed to sit down.

CHAPTER EIGHTEEN

A SET UP

As Dakota stood by with the camera, PaleoJoe, Shelly, and Karen began to carefully brush away dirt from the eggshell fossils. PaleoJoe motioned Dakota over and pointed to a bundle of fragments that he required a picture of. Carefully, Dakota focused the camera and remembering to keep his thumb well out of it, snapped the picture. While he was at it, he snapped a picture of Shelly too, down on her knees in the dirt holding her brush and intensely excited by her find. She never noticed.

And just when things didn't seem as though they could get any more exciting, Shelly let out a squeal that meant either she had been bitten by a deadly rattlesnake or that she had discovered something more.

She had discovered something more.

"Look, PaleoJoe! This one isn't broken!"

Everyone crowded around. Dakota found himself pushed and jostled this way and that until he almost fell over. Detective Franks appeared at his back and provided a prop. He was like a wall. Nothing could budge him.

"Thanks," said Dakota.

"No problem," said Detective Franks.

"Wow," said Mary Rodgers, flinging sweat from her eyes. "This is just simply astonishing."

"What is it?" asked Dakota.

"Dinosaur eggs," said Fred his eyes wide with disbelief.

"Yes, we knew that," said Dakota. "You mean more eggs?"

"He means unbroken dinosaur eggs!!" PaleoJoe exclaimed from where he was kneeling beside Shelly. "*Iguanodon* eyes! There is a nest of eggs here and some of them seem to be unbroken!"

"No one has ever found *Stegosaurus* eggs before," Fred explained to Dakota and Detective Franks. "And unbroken dinosaur eggs are rare. This is a fabulous find!"

There was a lot of shouting and hand-shaking and dancing about. Shelly, PaleoJoe, and Karen, their concentration unbroken, carefully continued to dig and brush around the find. Dakota glanced up once to see Buzzsaw, looking very thoughtful, standing apart from the others.

By the end of the day, a hot and tired but exultant team of diggers gathered under the canopy of the large open-sided tent.

"Well," PaleoJoe reported to everyone, "we have found what looks like a nest of *Stegosaurus* eggs. We found many egg fragments and 3 whole eggs!"

The people in the tent applauded.

"So, what I suggest we do is everyone go get cleaned up and then let's have supper in town to celebrate Shelly's find!"

More applause and people began scurrying for their tents. Dakota hung back and deliberately put himself in the path of Shelly.

"Hi, Shelly," he said. "I just wanted to say congratulations. You're like a real paleontologist now!"

"And you're like a real pain," said Shelly in her maximum unfriendly voice, brushing rudely past him. "I wish you would just go away!"

Dakota sighed and trudged back to his tent. He found it empty.

"Drat," he muttered to himself as he got out his backpack and began digging for a clean shirt. Why did girls have to be so difficult?

Then, as he rummaged in his bag he discovered something that made his knees start to shake and his stomach feel weird. And it wasn't a shirt.

He pulled out his hand and, as he feared, found that he was holding a handful of fossils. There was no doubt in his mind that he was holding fossils from the dig.

There was also no doubt in his mind who had put them in his backpack.

Dakota was sure, that for some reason, Buzzsaw was trying to plant these stolen things on Dakota. He wondered why the man would be trying to set him up like that. In any event, it was starting to make him mad.

CHAPTER NINETEEN

LEFT BEHIND

Quickly Dakota stashed the fossils back into his backpack. He did not want anyone to find him holding those! They would never ever believe him. He thought frantically for a minute about what he could do about this and suddenly a course of action came clear to him. He would have to put the fossils back in the dig. He would have to do it when no one was looking.

And the perfect time for that would be when everyone went into town to celebrate.

Without thinking about it too much, he ducked and slithered under his cot where he was completely hidden.

He rested quietly in the warm tent, smelling darkness, and he waited. Suddenly someone barged into the tent. He recognized Detective Franks when he called out.

"Dakota?"

Dakota kept still in the darkness.

PaleoJoe poked his head in. "Did you find him?" he asked.

"Ummm, no," said Detective Franks. "I think he must have hopped into one of the other cars. He'll be okay."

Detective Franks backed out of the tent. He could see the top of Dakota's foot as it peeked out from under the cot. Well, he thought, he wants to be alone for some reason. Better let him have his way.

Dakota heard the rustle of the tent flap as Detective Franks left. He never knew his secret was known. He could hear the voices of everyone as they loaded up. It was dusk by now and the light being somewhat dim, Dakota hoped that it would help people not to notice that he wasn't there.

Eventually he heard the engines start up and the chug of the vehicles as they pulled out of camp. The noise of the engines became faint. Soon Dakota knew he was alone.

He rolled out from under the cot.

105

In the dim twilight outside, the camp was deserted. It was eerily quiet with only the sound of a rising wind sighing across the open plain. Dakota thought he could hear his own heart thumping.

Overhead the sky was blanketed with a layer of clouds. Storm, thought Dakota. He knew the signs because he hated wild wind storms. Shelly probably loved them, he thought gloomily. That girl was never going to be friends with him.

Rule Number Twelve, Dakota invented as he walked toward the dig area. *Try not to care so much.*

He had the fossils in his pocket. As he approached the dig site, he paused to examine the eggs as they lay carefully exposed in their layers of rock and sand. Dakota remembered PaleoJoe saying that finding dinosaur eggs was always important because they could tell paleontologists a lot about the animal's growth and the family life of dinosaurs.

Walking silently around the rim of the dig site, Dakota made his way to the place where he had seen Buzzsaw standing when he had put something in his pockets. Carefully, Dakota looked around at the grid portion that had been assigned to Buzzsaw. He didn't think he could just toss the fossils back into the dirt.

Then he saw Buzzsaw's bucket carelessly left in the bottom of his excavation. It still contained dirt.

Perfect, thought Dakota.

There were three fossils. They were very small and appeared to be of some form of plant. Walking over to the half filled bucket, Dakota put the fossils in and pushed them down into the sandy dirt.

Now, he thought, all I have to do is to be sure someone sees him screen those tomorrow.

Just then, over the sound of the rising wind, Dakota heard the unmistakable drone of an airplane. Quickly he dashed back to the tents. Keeping close to the canvas sides he peered into the darkening sky as the sound of the plane came closer.

It was Crazy Chuck. Even in the darkening night, Dakota recognized the little yellow plane as it circled the camp and then began its landing on the little strip.

What should he do? Dakota did not want to be in the company of Crazy Chuck for any reason, let alone being caught by himself in camp. Hiding behind the tent, Dakota cautiously peered around the edge.

He couldn't see anything. The dig itself was

lost in shadows. Night had fallen and under the cloudy sky no moonlight illuminated anything.

Then Dakota saw a pinprick of light and realized that Crazy Chuck must have a flashlight with him. He watched as the light approached the dig site.

Dakota thought he could probably play hide and seek around the tents. If he was very quiet there was no reason for Chuck to think anyone was in camp in the first place.

But Chuck didn't come into the camp. Dakota watched as the light bobbed and wove its way to the dig site. He saw it pause for a very long time over the eggs.

And then it retreated. Crazy Chuck just walked back to his plane and in moments Dakota heard the cough of the engine as Chuck fired it up. The plane taxied out and with a roar took off and disappeared into the night.

CHAPTER TWENTY

CELEBRATION

Shelly bounced along in the Jeep beside Karen. In the back was the rather smelly Buzzsaw, but he was quiet and didn't say anything. Shelly decided that she preferred to have him instead of Dakota riding with them.

They reached the small town of Medicine Rock after about 15 minutes of rough and dusty jouncing about. They pulled in behind Fred's pickup just in time to hear PaleoJoe complaining about Fred hitting every bump and pothole in the road as he clambered out. Everyone gathered on the sidewalk outside the restaurant and that's when Shelly noticed Dakota wasn't with them.

"Where's Dakota?" she asked.

"He wasn't feeling well," said Detective Franks. "He said he wanted to go to bed early."

Shelly shrugged as they all trooped inside. At least she wouldn't have to try and ignore him all night. Sometimes that was hard to do.

Francine's was the small town's only diner. That night it was full of the regulars. Shelly and Karen entered and were greeted by the blare of country music from a jukebox in the corner. A group of young men were clustered around a pool table laughing and joking as they spun the balls into the pockets of the table. A TV mounted in a corner near the ceiling silently scrolled the news of the day underneath a talking head whose voice was muffled in the general roar and talk of the busy diner.

PaleoJoe and his crew gathered in a little side room that had a long table in it designed to hold a large group. Everyone took seats and Linda, the waitress, came to get orders. Steak was the traditional food of celebration, so that's what they ordered. Shelly ordered a chocolate milkshake too.

When the drinks came, PaleoJoe rose to make a toast.

"To Shelly and her great discovery!" he said.

"To Shelly!" everyone echoed.

Shelly slurped her milkshake and felt very happy.

Over dinner PaleoJoe told Shelly about dinosaur eggs.

"The first and biggest was found in France around 1869," he said sawing into his steak. "It was football shaped and was about one foot long, ten inches wide and could hold a half gallon of liquid. We don't know for sure, but it may have weighed up to fifteen-and-a-half pounds!"

"Wow," said Shelly, impressed as she slurped her milkshake. Her eggs were not that big, but she still knew how impressive her find was going to be.

"You know," said PaleoJoe thoughtfully, "there have been many dinosaur eggs found, but rarely do the eggs have preserved parts of embryos in them. Without an embryo it is difficult to match the egg with the species."

"So even if we found these eggs with the bones of a *Stegosaurus,* that doesn't mean they are the eggs of a *Stegosaurus*?" asked Shelly.

"That's right," said PaleoJoe. "Are you interested in hearing a story?"

"Is it about dinosaur eggs?"

"Of course!"

"Then tell away, oh great paleontologist!" Shelly giggled.

And so as dessert and coffee were being served, PaleoJoe told everyone a story about dinosaur eggs. Intent on the story, no one noticed when Buzzsaw slipped away to make a phone call.

CHAPTER TWENTY-ONE

PALEOJOE'S STORY

"In 1922 a paleontologist by the name of Roy Chapman Andrews took a heroic expedition to the Gobi desert looking for fossils," began PaleoJoe.

"Why was it heroic?" Shelly interrupted. She spooned a delicious chunk of chocolate cake into her mouth.

"You obviously know very little about the Gobi desert of 1922 or you wouldn't ask that question," said PaleoJoe.

Shelly stuck out a chocolate coated tongue at him. "You know I know very little about the Gobi desert or any desert of 1922. As you will

recall, I am not as old as you."

Shelly giggled when she saw she had scored with that one.

"First, they had to contend with extreme climate conditions. There was intense heat during the day..."

Detective Franks grunted sympathetically.

"...and intense cold during the nights. There were monster sandstorms that could bury an entire camp under tons of glass-sharp, suffocating sand in a matter of mere minutes.

"And then there were bandits. Just like today, there are always bad guys who try to steal the artifacts, fossils, and treasures of scientists and scholars who hunt for the past. China controlled Inner Mongolia and they were engaged in civil wars. Russia controlled Outer Mongolia and they were recovering from revolution. So you see there were a lot of people with guns roaming about and not a lot of anyone to stop them.

"And then there were things like poisonous snakes. These were deadly. They could make a man very sick or even kill him if they bit him."

"Okay," said Shelly in agreement. "This was definitely a heroic adventure."

"They must have been looking for something really important to risk all of that," said Mary Rodgers from where she was, leaning forward, her elbows on the table, listening to every word.

PaleoJoe smiled a mysterious smile. "Only fossils," he said.

"I can understand," said Shelly. "I'd brave bandits and poisonous snakes to find fossils."

"Me too," said Karen. "Especially if you found dinosaur eggs!"

"Right!" Shelly agreed enthusiastically.

"And so," continued PaleoJoe, "on July 13, 1923, out on the Flaming Cliffs of Shabarak Usu, Roy Chapman Andrews found just that."

"Dinosaur eggs?" Shelly's eyes were wide with excitement.

"Dinosaur eggs," said PaleoJoe. "Weathering out of the sandstone rock of the Cretaceous period were shell fragments and 3 eggs."

"Just like what I found," said Shelly.

"Very similar," agreed PaleoJoe. "But you see in 1923 paleontologists did not know if baby dinosaurs were hatched from eggs or if they were born live. This find would allow them to determine that it appears that dinosaurs laid eggs and their young were hatched."

"Cool," said Shelly.

"But that isn't all they found," said

115

PaleoJoe. "They also found the body of a small toothless dinosaur on top of the nest. They called it *Oviraptor* and determined that it had been trying to steal the eggs to eat. It took scientists 50 years to discover that the *Oviraptor* wasn't stealing those eggs, it was protecting them!"

"Awesome," Shelly pronounced. "Now tell us more about the heroics."

"Well," said PaleoJoe. "One night the temperature in the camp dropped to near freezing. Suddenly snakes began to invade the camp by the dozens. They were attracted to the light and the warmth. They began to turn up everywhere. Men found them coiled in their hats and the cook found one in bed with him! When Andrews stepped out of his tent to see if more were coming, he stepped on a rope, thought it was a snake, and nearly jumped out of his skin. It was amazing, but no one was bit and after two nights of the snake invasion Andrews decided to break camp before anyone did get bit.

"And then one of the men of the expedition looked up into the sky to see a giant tawny cloud heading their way. It was a monster sandstorm. When it struck, Andrews said his pajama top was torn from his back and then lashed at by the sand. Those storms could be very very fierce."

Just as he concluded his story Linda, their

waitress, came in to clear away plates and to see if there was anything else anyone wanted.

"So you've heard about the storm, then?" she asked PaleoJoe.

"What storm?" PaleoJoe asked, startled.

"It's on the TV right now. You can see for yourself. Big storm headed this way. Thought you diggers would want to come in off the plains before it hits."

PaleoJoe and Fred almost collided with each other in their hurry to see the TV broadcast. A few minutes later when they returned to the table they looked very worried indeed.

"There is a big storm headed this way," PaleoJoe confirmed. "It should hit sometime tomorrow. We won't be safe on the plains in our tents. So, everyone knows what to do. We've got to secure the site and then get ourselves safe. We better leave now."

They paid their bill and everyone rushed out to the waiting vehicles to make the short but dark and bumpy ride back to camp.

CHAPTER TWENTY-TWO

DAKOTA'S PLAN

The first thing Shelly did when they got back to camp was look to make sure her tool roll was where she had left it. It was. Then she went to find Dakota to see what he had been up to. She didn't find him, but she found PaleoJoe.

"Dakota didn't go into town with us," she said.

"I know," said PaleoJoe. "Look, Shelly, you are being pretty hard on that kid. Why don't you see if you can cut him some slack?"

Shelly snorted in annoyance. "Not likely."

PaleoJoe sighed. "Pish. In any case, you should go get some sleep. There are only just a few hours until dawn. We are going to have to work like maniacs to get this site secure."

"Okay," Shelly agreed. As she headed back to her tent she noticed for the first time the rising wind and the darkness of the starless sky.

Meanwhile, Dakota had wasted no time in finding Detective Franks on his return and pulled him aside. He told him everything from finding the fossils, to hiding under his cot, to the visit from Crazy Chuck.

Detective Franks listened without interrupting.

"I was afraid of something like this," he said when Dakota finished. "PaleoJoe allows anyone on these digs. I've told him about it before, but he won't be careful."

"I don't trust that Buzzsaw guy," said Dakota. "I don't like the way he keeps waving and winking at me as though I were part of his little scheme."

Suddenly Dakota had an idea. "Hey, that's it!" he said snapping his fingers.

"What's it?" asked Detective Franks suspiciously.

"For some reason Buzzsaw wants to involve me with his stealing," said Dakota excitedly. "Well, I'll let him! Or at least I will pretend to let him. I'll go undercover."

"Now hold on," said Detective Franks. "First of all, Buzzsaw is probably just trying to set you up to be the fall guy. He's going to be taking some fossils and it would be to his advantage if everyone thought you had done it."

"Maybe," said Dakota. "But he did say he wanted to talk to me later. I think this is our chance to find out what he's up to."

"I don't like it," said Detective Franks.

"There's nothing to it," said Dakota. "Everyone is all around here. I'll just talk to him and see if I can get an idea of his plans. This will work!"

And maybe, thought Dakota, I can prove to Shelly and everyone that I can do something worthwhile and not just be a mess-up all the time.

"Absolutely not," said Detective Franks. "Under no circumstances are you to do anything of the sort. If Buzzsaw is up to something bad, I don't want you anywhere near it. Understand?"

But before Dakota could argue further, PaleoJoe found them and ordered them to bed.

The storm was approaching.

CHAPTER TWENTY-THREE

THE STORM

The first brightening of morning was barely visible when the camp burst into frantic activity. PaleoJoe was concerned about heavy rains. He was also a little worried about possible flooding of the site. Everyone knew that the dinosaur bones were fragile. They could suffer damage from the storm if they weren't properly protected.

The biggest worry was the eggs.

Shelly and Karen worked side by side in the excavation. Shelly took orders from Karen. They worked quickly and carefully. First, they placed plaster casts on as many of the exposed

bones as they could find. The plaster would be just like a jacket and protect the bones just as a plaster cast protects a broken arm.

Shelly placed wet paper towels over the exposed bones as well as a bit of the surrounding dirt. Next, a layer a tinfoil went over that. Dakota cut burlap sacks into long, wide strips while Karen mixed the plaster in a medium-sized bucket. She used her hands to mix plaster powder and water together until she had a thick paste.

Dakota handed the burlap strips to Shelly who took them without comment, but also managed to not scowl either. She placed the burlap strips into the bucket of plaster until they were all mushy and soggy. Then they pulled the strips out and placed them as the top layer on the foil covered bones. They created several layers to make sure the jacket was sturdy.

Meanwhile, PaleoJoe and Fred were working on the eggs, creating not only plaster casts, but also covering them with a sturdy low frame which they made as windproof and waterproof as they could.

When all the plastering was completed, everyone helped put down large sheets of plastic and tarps. They covered as much of the dig site as possible. The corners were staked and the team put a layer of dirt on the tarps to hold them down. Another, heavier layer of dirt went around the edges.

As the team took down the tents it began to rain. Large fat raindrops began scattering over the dry ground. This was only the very edge of the big storm but it was time to leave. Everyone piled into the vehicles and this time Dakota made certain he was not left behind. In fact, he boldly hopped into the back of the pickup truck with the piles of collapsed tents and the odoriferous Buzzsaw.

As they jounced away from the camp Dakota saw that Buzzsaw was watching him. Carefully, so as not to be thrown from the bouncing bed of the truck, Dakota crawled his way over to Buzzsaw and sat down next to him. They leaned with their backs against the cab. They were somewhat protected from the dollops of rain as the truck blundered its way forward.

"I think I have something of yours," said Dakota. He put his hand in his pocket and brought out the three fossils that he had found in his backpack. After formulating his undercover plan, Dakota had retrieved the fossils from the bucket where he had put them earlier. He needed them for his plan.

Buzzsaw quickly took the fossils and put

them in his pocket. A wicked smile flickered across his face.

"Geez, kid," he said. "You took long enough. I was beginning to think we had made a mistake about you."

"No mistake," said Dakota with more bravery in his voice then he actually felt.

"Yeah, I figured that out when you didn't go to the celebration dinner. You stayed behind to snoop, didn't you?"

Dakota just nodded as the safest response.

"Well, whatever little treasures you found to keep are yours and I won't tell anyone."

"Thanks," said Dakota. "Um, you said we needed to talk?"

Buzzsaw smiled again. "Yeah, we need to talk, but not here. Listen—when we get into town, I'd like to take you on a little tour of things. That sound interesting to you?"

"Sure," said Dakota, as sure as he could be that there wasn't anything that sounded less interesting as far as he was concerned.

"Good. Man, Crazy Chuck sure had you pinned right. You're going to love this, Spike. You're going to love this."

And so, Spike, A.K.A. Dakota Jackson, undercover, jounced and bounced alongside a master criminal while the sky became the color of mud and thunder rumbled in the distance.

CHAPTER TWENTY-FOUR

DAKOTA DISAPPEARS

PaleoJoe and his crew had to take refuge in town from storms before. Whenever they did they stayed with Mabel Winters, a retired librarian who owned a huge house with rooms to rent.

Everyone had to pair up and in a move that surprised Dakota, as well as everyone else, he volunteered to share a room with Buzzsaw.

"Birds of a feather," thought Shelly sourly as she watched the two disappear into their room.

Detective Franks, who knew what Dakota was up to, did not like this arrangement at all.

But, later, when he set out to look for Dakota, he couldn't find him. He couldn't find Buzzsaw either.

"Detective Franks!" Shelly said, stopping him in the living room. She seemed upset.

"What's wrong, Shelly?"

Outside the old house the storm was moving in. Thunder rumbled and flashes of lightning lit the old ripples in the window. It had begun to rain a little harder now but this, still, was not the main brunt of the storm.

"Dakota has taken my cell phone!"

"What? How do you know it was Dakota?"

"Because he left a note," Shelly said angrily, and showed Detective Franks the note she had discovered in her backpack.

It was written in pencil and it said:

Shelly,
I'm sorry I had to
borrow your cell phone.
Please tell
Detective Franks I took it.
I'll get it back to you
real soon.
Dakota

"I wish PaleoJoe had never asked that boy to come!" stomped Shelly. "He always has to take things. It's why he is in trouble at school all the time! He's such a jerk."

"I'm glad you showed this to me, Shelly," said Detective Franks. "I wish Dakota had not borrowed your phone either because I am afraid he is doing something extremely dangerous."

Startled out of her angry outburst by his serious expression, Shelly was suddenly sure there was something going on that she was missing.

"What's going on, Detective Franks? There is something mysterious happening and I want to know what it is."

"Well, come along with me then," said Detective Franks. "We need to go find my old friend Constable James. He's the chief of police here."

"Is Dakota really in that big of trouble?" asked Shelly, suddenly picturing Dakota behind bars in the town's jail.

"He's in trouble all right," said Detective Franks. "Come on. We need to find PaleoJoe. I'll tell you both about it on the way."

CHAPTER TWENTY-FIVE

BECKY'S ROCK SHOP

Dakota knew all about Shelly's pink space-age cell phone because he had overheard her explaining it to Karen. He knew she could access the internet with it, that it could take pictures, and that she had pretty good coverage with it. He knew that she had the cell phone numbers of both Detective Franks and PaleoJoe programmed into it.

He also knew she would never let him borrow it. That's why he took it. And he thought, being honest with himself, there is no rule to cover this because I did take it even though I'm going to give it back.

He stuck it into his back pocket and headed out into the storm with Buzzsaw who wanted to take him on a "little tour."

The "little tour" ended up to be a mad dash through the rain the full length of Main Street, which brought them to a small, shabby shop at the edge of town with a sign above the door that said **Becky's Rock Shop.** There was a closed sign in the window but when Buzzsaw knocked, the door flew open. He and Dakota stumbled inside, dripping wet. Dakota had no idea what was going on.

The woman who had opened the door for them slammed it shut behind them. Dakota found he was in a small, cramped shop. Every inch of space was filled with bins and shelves full of and covered with rocks.

"Come into the back," said the woman, leading the way behind the sales counter.

Dakota followed Buzzsaw through a small door behind the counter and into a brightly lit room. A small table covered with more rocks stood in the center of the little room. A refrigerator and sink lined against the wall next to a back door. Four chairs were arranged around the table. Sitting in one of them was Crazy Chuck. It looked like he was playing a game of Solitaire.

"About time you showed up," he said, thumping down a couple of cards.

"Oh, you're dripping all over everything!"
said the woman to Dakota and Buzzsaw.

She was short and heavyset with sharply
curled bronze hair. She wore a lot of makeup.
"Buzzsaw, get a towel. You're making a mess."

Buzzsaw dug in a nearby cupboard and came up with a couple of not so clean looking towels. He tossed one to Dakota and briefly ran the other over his head in an effort to soak up most of the drips. Dakota did the same.

"Okay," Buzzsaw said. "I'm here now. Is everything set?"

"Everything is set," said Crazy Chuck. He picked up a couple of cards which were face down and looked at what they were. Dakota realized he was cheating! Did it make any sense to cheat yourself at cards? he wondered.

"We just need to leave real soon or that storm is going to make things tough."

"We have time," said Buzzsaw.

"What's up with the kid?" asked the woman.

"Name's Spike," Buzzsaw introduced Dakota. "He's going to help us here. Look after the shop while we go get the stuff."

"I see," said the woman, looking Dakota over as though he were a particularly nasty insect she intended to squash.

"Better show him what to do," said Buzzsaw.

"Nobody is going to come into the shop in the middle of this downpour," said the woman. "I don't think we need him."

131

"Still," said Buzzsaw. "It wouldn't look good if the shop is closed when the crime is committed, now would it?"

"Come on kid," the woman motioned with a plump hand decorated with blood red nails.

Dakota followed the woman back into the shop. She flipped on a couple of lights revealing her untidy shop full of rocks. Only now Dakota could see that it wasn't just rocks that were for sale in this shop. There were also fossils.

"My shop," said the woman.

"Are you Becky?" asked Dakota.

"Most of the time," she answered. "Look, all you got to do is stand here behind the counter and if anyone comes in to buy a rock just sell it to them."

"Okay," said Dakota.

Becky went to the door and flipped over the closed sign so it read OPEN.

A sudden clap of thunder rattled the panes in the window.

"Hairy monkeys, look at it rain," said the woman peering out the shop window.

"Hey Bec, ya got any food in this dump?" Buzzsaw said from the back room.

"In the fridge," Becky squalled back. "You just stand here then," she said to Dakota. "We'll be going in a few minutes."

"Right."

Dakota stood behind the counter until Becky had gone into the other room. Then he began to look around. The fossils he saw all looked like regular small fossils anyone could find. There were a couple of bigger fossils in a locked case at the back of the room that looked like they might be bones. He quickly snapped a couple of pictures of them with Shelly's phone.

One thing was sure, Buzzsaw and his friends were planning on going somewhere to steal something. Dakota had no intention of being left behind to guard the shop.

CHAPTER TWENTY-SIX

CRAZY CHUCK RIDES A STORM

Dakota was not exactly sure how he had managed it, but after about twenty minutes Becky left him on duty in the rock shop Dakota found himself in the back of Crazy Chuck's airplane, frantically hiding under a pile of tarps he found in the back.

His ally had been the storm.

A monster crack of thunder and a huge flash of lightning resulted in the lights going out in the shop. Quickly Dakota went to the front door, opened it, and allowed it to bang close. He then ducked behind a tall display of rocks and hid. Everyone thought he had run out into the rain.

Everyone ran out to try and catch him.

As they did that, Dakota had ducked into the back room and slipped out the door he had seen there earlier. He discovered that he was in a sort of garage or shed and that there was an old pickup truck parked there. Thinking that this would be the vehicle they would use to get to the plane, he hid himself in the bed of the truck under the pile of boxes and junk that cluttered the back.

He had been right. Only a few minutes later, Chuck and Buzzsaw came out, got in the truck and drove off. It was cold and wet in the back, but Dakota stayed hidden.

Getting into the plane had been a trick. At first he didn't think he was going to be able to, but then there had been just a moment when both Chuck and Buzzsaw had gone around the small building and disappeared inside.

Dakota put on the speed, and ran out to where the plane waited in the steady downpour of rain. He popped inside Crazy Chuck's plane, dived into the back cargo area and covered up with the tarp. Quickly, he then whipped out

135

Shelly's cell phone and selected the number for Detective Franks.

He answered on the first ring.

"Franks," he voice was tense and gruff.

"This is Dakota," Dakota whispered hoarsely.

"Where are you?" Franks demanded. "You get on back here right now, Dakota. You're getting yourself in way over your head."

"Only have a minute," Dakota whispered again. "I'm following Buzzsaw. He's on his way to steal something. He has something to do with Becky's Rock Shop. Uh oh, gotta go."

Dakota had heard the raised voices of Crazy Chuck and Buzzsaw as they came through the downpour of rain. Soon they were both inside and Crazy Chuck was starting the engine.

And then Dakota discovered why Chuck was called *Crazy*.

The little plane buffeted and leaped down the runway. The rain smashed and spattered against the windshield. And when the plane jumped into the air, the wind slammed into it and tossed it about like a small bird trying to fight a very big wind.

Chuck did some fancy swerving and Dakota thought he could hear Buzzsaw laughing like a maniac on a murderous carnival ride. And that's what it felt like. The rain smashed into the plane with a deafening roar. Lightning zigged-zapped just beyond the windows. The plane thumped in the air as though it were being hammered by a giant fist.

Dakota thought he would probably die.

CHAPTER TWENTY-SEVEN

SHELLY WORKS IT OUT

"Blast that boy!" Detective Franks was mad at Dakota because he was worried about him.

"What is it?" asked Shelly. "What did he say?"

PaleoJoe, Detective Franks, and Shelly were all sitting in the office of Constable James. Constable James was a tall, thin man, slightly bald, with very blue eyes. Shelly liked him right away. He reminded her of a friendly ostrich with his scrawny neck and graying hair.

"He didn't tell me where he was," said Detective Franks in frustration.

"Is he okay?" asked PaleoJoe.

"He seems to be. For now. He said he was following Buzzsaw. He said something about a rock shop at the edge of town."

"I know the place," said Constable James. "I've had my eye on it for some time. I think they deal fossils on the black market, but I haven't been able to prove anything."

"Well, we're pretty sure Buzzsaw is involved with stealing fossils," said PaleoJoe. "When we searched his room we found a whole bunch of fossils and even some bones from the dig."

"Dakota seemed to think Buzzsaw was getting ready to steal something really big," said Franks.

"Like what?" asked Constable James. "Could he be after any of those *Stegosaurus* bones you found at that dig?"

"It isn't likely," aid PaleoJoe. "They are all in plaster jackets and most of them are pretty big."

"He's after the eggs," said Shelly. "That must be it, PaleoJoe! He's after the dinosaur eggs!"

PaleoJoe slapped his forehead. "That's it! You've got to be right, Shelly."

"But how could he get them in this storm?" asked Constable James. "The road is too muddy

in this storm—they couldn't take a truck. He would need an airplane to get to the site. Who would be crazy enough to fly in this storm?"

"CRAZY CHUCK!" said PaleoJoe, Detective Franks, and Shelly all at the same time.

"And I bet Dakota has gone along for the ride," said Shelly grimly.

CHAPTER TWENTY-EIGHT

THE THEFT

The wind was a howling fury as Dakota left the airplane following Buzzsaw and Crazy Chuck after they landed. He knew right away where they were and he knew exactly what Buzzsaw was going to steal.

He hunkered down close to ground and watched as the two men ransacked the dig, uprooting tarps and exposing the carefully plastered bones to the lash of the wind and rain. When they came to where PaleoJoe and Fred had enclosed the eggs, they quickly kicked apart the protective covering. Using tools they began to extract the eggs from the ground.

Dakota thought frantically, but he didn't see what he could do. He would be no match for the two men and he just didn't see anyway he could stop them. He took out Shelly's phone and snapped some pictures of the theft. He was pretty far away and in the middle of a fairly heavy storm, but it was all he could think to try.

Quickly he made his way back to the plane and climbed into the back. He made a little barricade over himself to protect him when the stolen fossils would be loaded in. He thought he was well hidden. He hoped that Buzzsaw and Crazy Chuck would be in too much of a hurry to really notice anything anyway.

Then he flipped open Shelly's phone and called Detective Franks.

"Dakota?" Franks answered immediately.

"I'm in Crazy Chuck's plane," said Dakota breathlessly. "Tell PaleoJoe that they are ripping up the site. They are trying to steal the eggs! I don't know what to do to stop them. Shelly is going to be so upset!"

"Never mind about that," said Franks. "Listen, are you hidden now?"

"Yeah. I'm on the plane," Dakota said. He couldn't believe it, but he was almost crying. How could he be so helpless as to allow those thieves to tear up the dig site like that?

"Dakota!" Franks' harsh voice focused his attention. "Just stay out of sight. Leave the phone on. We'll be able to track you. When you land..."

And that's when the batteries on Shelly's space-age cell phone went dead.

"There wasn't a full charge on it when he took it," said Shelly in a stricken voice.

"Well, we know he's okay right now. What we don't know is where they will take the fossils next," said Detective Franks.

"Actually," said Constable James. "I might have an idea about that."

Dakota held the dead phone in his hand staring in disbelief.

Rule number Thirteen: Never trust your life to technology. That's a great rule to be unlucky number thirteen, he thought glumly.

Just then the doors of the plane slammed open. Buzzsaw and Crazy Chuck began loading in bundles and crates of stolen fossils. Dakota kept very still.

They never knew he was there.

CHAPTER TWENTY-NINE

CAPTURE AND ESCAPE

The wind was still strong as they took to the air once again. Dakota was beginning to feel as though he would never, ever again voluntarily get on a carnival ride. Then he felt the plane descend. They taxied over some very rough ground. Crazy Chuck must have driven the plane into a shelter of some sort because all of a sudden the crashing roar of rain stopped.

The plane also came to a stop. The whirr of the propellers died away. Buzzsaw and Crazy Chuck began to unload the crates and bundles from around Dakota. They were almost finished when Crazy Chuck reached in thinking that

Dakota was one of the bundles of stolen fossils and discovered his mistake.

"Spike! You tricky rascal," he exclaimed, catching Dakota by his ankle and pulling him out.

Dakota was all tangled up in the tarp, so it was easy for Crazy Chuck to trip him up. Dakota sprawled on the floor and discovered that they were in some sort of barn. The floor was covered with bits and wisps of old hay and piles of other old stuff, left behind by long ago horses, cows, and their owners.

"Hey, Buzzsaw," yelled Crazy Chuck. "We have company."

Buzzsaw came over to investigate. When he saw Dakota sprawled on the floor tangled helplessly in the tarp, he slapped his knee and laughed hard and loud.

"Oh, Spike," he said. "I knew you would come in handy."

Crazy Chuck reached down and hefted Dakota over his shoulder. The men left the barn and headed across a farmyard overgrown with weeds toward a very ancient looking farmhouse. There was a lull in the storm and while the wind still blew, the rain had stopped for a moment. Everything was wet and the dirt driveway leading into the yard was filled with muddy potholes.

145

Crazy Chuck took Dakota inside and dumped him on a chair in what was probably the old kitchen. There appeared to be no electricity in the place because Buzzsaw was lighting a kerosene lamp. Crazy Chuck had found a hank of old rope and he was tying Dakota to his chair, tarp and all.

"Well, we pulled that one off!" said Buzzsaw rubbing his hands together. "And I only had to pretend to be that fish-faced paleontologist's assistant for a few weeks. It wasn't so bad."

Dakota assumed he was referring to PaleoJoe.

"We should move the stuff out as soon as possible, though," said Crazy Chuck. "You didn't count on the fish-faced paleontologist to bring along a detective." Buzzsaw had discovered that Mr. Franks was really Detective Franks when he faked being asleep the night Shelly's tool roll was stolen: he had also told Crazy Chuck.

"Or a sassy little girl or a nosey little boy," said Buzzsaw smacking Dakota in the back of the head. "But you're right. I'll call Becky and arrange for an earlier pickup. And then you and I can disappear."

Buzzsaw flipped out his own cell phone, batteries apparently charged, and punched in a number. He listened, but there didn't appear to be any answer from the other end.

"I don't like this," he said, nervously re-punching in the number. "Becky said she would be waiting by the phone for our call."

Again there was no answer.

"What do you think we ought to do?" asked Buzzsaw.

But before he could answer, another sound was added to the moaning of the wind and the creaking of the old house. It was the sound of police sirens.

A lot of police sirens.

Crazy Chuck and Buzzsaw were galvanized into panic action. With more presence of mind Buzzsaw broke out through a window in a small side room, but Crazy Chuck got too close to Dakota who toppled his chair over in his path. Crazy Chuck tripped and banged his head hard enough on the floor that Dakota was sure he was seeing bright flashes of stars. The crash stunned him enough so that by the time Constable James and his men discovered them, Dakota had trapped a very angry and very loud Crazy Chuck beneath his chair.

147

CHAPTER THIRTY

THE OLD MILLER PLACE

One of the police officers had just managed to get Dakota untangled from his tarp and rope when Shelly burst into the room.

She was dripping water from her pink raincoat and there was mud on her pink boots, but when she saw Dakota she didn't hesitate to fling herself at him catching him in a bear hug.

"Ooof!" said Dakota, feeling all the breath squeezed out of him.

"DAKOTA!" Shelly yelled, and maybe someone in China didn't quite hear her. "Are you okay? Are you hurt? Did you catch those brainless thieves? Where's my phone?"

Dakota, feeling a little dizzy and overwhelmed, picked his chair up off the floor and sat on it. The room was spinning a bit but he could see police officers handcuffing Crazy Chuck and taking him away.

"It's here," he said, fumbling in his back pocket. He pulled out the cell phone and handed it to Shelly. "The batteries died. I'm sorry."

"It's my fault," said Shelly. "I should have charged them before you borrowed it. Next time I'll make sure."

Next time? Had Dakota heard her right?

Detective Franks came in. "Well, it looks like Buzzsaw got away. Are you hurt at all, Dakota?"

"No sir," said Dakota, wondering when people were going to start yelling at him, although the buzzing in his ears was becoming quite loud, so maybe he wouldn't hear them.

"Well, that was a pretty stupid thing to do," said Detective Franks.

"It was a brave thing to do," said Shelly.

Did Shelly call him brave? Dakota felt hot and his head was swimming. He wasn't sure he was hearing things right.

"Okay, Shelly. I can see he's had a hard time of it. We'll talk about it later."

Detective Franks turned away to see to the arrest of Crazy Chuck when PaleoJoe entered the room.

"Constable James was right," he said. "The old Miller place. Deserted farmhouse and barn. Perfect for storing stolen fossils. This place was definitely being used as a clearing house for fossils heading for the black market. That old barn is full of stuff."

"What about the eggs?" asked Shelly anxiously.

"The eggs are there all right," said PaleoJoe. "And the good news is that they look undamaged."

Oh, that's good, thought Dakota as he slipped off his chair and promptly passed out.

CHAPTER THIRTY-ONE

STEGOSAURUS EGGS

The grand opening for the *Stegosaurus* eggs was at the Balboa Museum. Dakota came with Detective Franks who had picked him up at home. Once again Dakota had spiked his hair. It was in honor of the *Stegosaurus*, he had told his mom. He felt it to be appropriate. But he was dressed up pretty nicely in a suit and tie.

The museum was full of people, many of whom came up to shake Dakota's hand. Fred Parkhurst gave him a thump on the back. He saw John and Mary Rodgers talking to a group of kids about digging fossils. Mary gave him a wave.

And finally he saw Shelly. She was dressed in a pink pant suit and her hair was caught in its pony tail with a pink ribbon. She was talking to Karen Orchard, but when she saw Dakota she came over to him right away.

"You look spiffy," she said.

"Thanks," said Dakota. "So do you."

"Do you want me to call you Spike, then?" she asked, gently tapping his spiked hairdo with the palm of her hand.

"Absolutely not!" he exclaimed. "I just thought it would be a tribute to our dinosaur."

Shelly laughed. "I agree," she said.

They were joined by PaleoJoe who was sipping punch from a paper cup.

"Come on over here, you two," he said. "I want you to see the display."

The dinosaur eggs were arranged on a velvet covered pedestal in the center space of the exhibit hall. They were roped off by thick, red silk ropes. Three uniformed guards, courtesy of Detective Franks, guarded the exhibit.

A lot of people were thronged around the exhibit. As Dakota followed PaleoJoe and Shelly through the mobs of milling people, he thought he caught sight of a man in the crowd that reminded him of someone.

And was that a whiff of smelly gym shoes?

He stopped and looked carefully around him, but the man had disappeared and the smell must have been his imagination.

"Come on, Dakota," said Shelly, impatiently grabbing him by the hand and hauling him through the crowd to stand by PaleoJoe at the front of the display.

A plaque in curly lettering read:

Stegosaurus eggs
Found in
South Dakota by
Shelly Brooks

Arranged around the plaque were a dozen or so pictures taken by Dakota at the dig site.

"Wow," said Shelly, smiling at Dakota and squeezing his hand. "It's perfect."

And Dakota thought that maybe it was.

The End

About PaleoJoe

PaleoJoe is a real paleontologist whose
recent adventures included digging in the famous
Como Bluff for *Allosaurus, Camptosaurus,* and
Apatosaurus.

A graduate of Niagara University, just outside
of the fossil rich Niagara Falls and Lewiston area
of New York, Joseph has collected fossils since
he was 10 years old. He has gone on digs around
the United States and abroad, hunting for dinosaur
fossils with some of the most famous and respected
paleontologists in the world. He is a member of
the Paleontological Research Institute and Society
of Vertebrate Paleontology and is the winner of the
prestigious Katherine Palmer Award for his work
communicating dinosaur and fossil information with
children and communities. He has given over 300
school presentations around the country.

He is also the author of *The Complete Guide
to Michigan Fossils* and *Hidden Dinosaurs.*

About Wendy Caszatt-Allen

Wendy Caszatt-Allen is an author, poet, playwright, and teacher. She is a graduate from the prestigious Interlochen Center for the Arts and Michigan State University. She is currently finishing her PhD in Language, Literacy, and Culture at the University of Iowa.

She is releasing *The Adventures of Pachelot: The Last Voyage of the Griffon* and *The Beaver Wars* in early 2007 with Mackinac Island Press.